A SCANDALOUS AFFAIR

It began as an innocent flirtation and likely would have remained so had dazzlingly beautiful opera singer Marissa Merrilli and her lovestruck young lord been left to their own devices. But a meddling family and a notorious gossip combined to drive Marissa into an aristocratic entanglement she had never desired. Still, everything might have worked out eventually if not for the unexpected interference of wealthy, debonair Gervase Maxwell. Gervase's erroneous assumption that Marissa was a fortune-hunting woman of easy virtue was a clarion call to battle that the volatile, headstrong singer could not ignore—and an unforgivable mistake she swore to make Mr. Maxwell pay for dearly . . .

The
Rose Domino

The
Rose Domino

by
Sheila Walsh

A SIGNET BOOK

NEW AMERICAN LIBRARY

A DIVISION OF PENGUIN BOOKS USA INC.

SIGNET TRADEMARK REG. U.S. PAT. OFF. AND FOREIGN COUNTRIES
REGISTERED TRADEMARK—MARCA REGISTRADA
HECHO EN DRESDEN, TN, U.S.A.

SIGNET, SIGNET CLASSIC, MENTOR, ONYX, PLUME, MERIDIAN
and NAL BOOKS are published by New American Library, a division of
Penguin Books USA Inc., 1633 Broadway, New York, New York 10019

First Printing, October, 1981

5 6 7 8 9 10 11 12 13

PRINTED IN THE UNITED STATES OF AMERICA

Chapter 1

An elegant black high-perch phaeton with gleaming
white wheels entered Hill Street at a spanking pace.
The gentleman in command of the ribbons handled
his team of matched grays with an easy confidence
that made his arrival a pleasure to behold, prompting
Miss Emily Phipps, who just happened to be glancing
out of her front drawing-room window at the time, to
confide to her sister that Mr. Maxwell must be returned from his travels for he had this very moment
arrived at Lady Kilroy's door.

Such a fine, distinguished gentleman—she sighed—
and so handsome! Lady Kilroy was indeed fortunate.
Oblivious of Hester's caustic rejoinder, she pressed
one hand to her gently palpitating bosom as the object of her admiration surrendered the reins into the
care of his groom and stepped lightly down. A long,
drab driving coat enveloped his tall slim figure, bil-
lowing out behind him as he moved swiftly across the
pavement. In the instant before he was lost to view
beneath the portico of the house next door, a shaft of
spring sunshine slanted beneath the brim of his hat to
touch the silver wings which nowadays graced his
dark hair.

Not by so much as a whisker did Gervase Maxwell
betray that he had noted that telltale flutter of the
curtain, but he was smiling faintly as the door was
opened to him.

"Her ladyship at home, is she?" he inquired casu-

1

ally of the footman, shrugging himself out of his coat without waiting for answer. The footman, only two months in his job, might have been thrown into confusion by this unlooked-for familiarity on the part of a complete stranger, but for the timely arrival of the butler.

Sair, showing that degree of privilege borne of a long acquaintance with Mr. Maxwell, accorded him one of his rare smiles and said how very agreeable it was to have him safe at home from foreign parts after all his jaunterings, and looking, "if you'll pardon the liberty, sir," exceedingly fit into the bargain.

Gervase thanked him gravely and hoped that Sir Edward and Lady Kilroy were likewise in prime twig.

"Tolerable, sir. Quite tolerable. Young Miss Eliza took a nasty dose of the measles not a month since which had us all in a pucker for a time, but she is mending splendidly now, so much so that Sir Edward has taken both her, and Miss Clara, this very day to stay with her laydship's mother down at Mancroft." Sair was further moved to confide judiciously that her ladyship was a trifle down-pin, what with one thing and another. "Howsoever, sir, your visit will be just the thing to have her in spirits again."

"Why, so I trust." Gervase set his hand on the rail of the scrolled ironwork banister. "You need not trouble to announce me, Sair."

"Very good, sir. You will find her ladyship in the small drawing room."

On the upper landing Gervase opened a door quietly upon a charming room where a very pretty lady occupied the chintz-covered sofa nearest the window, her enchanting profile bent in fierce concentration over a piece of needlework.

"Such industry," he murmured, gently mocking.

At the sound of his lazy, resonant voice she looked

2

up with a joyful cry, cast aside her sewing, and sprang to her feet, arms outflung in welcome. "Dearest Gervase—I knew you would not fail me!"

This blithe declaration of faith, though touching, prompted him to say, "I hope I may never hear myself accused of that, my dear!"

He crossed the room to take the hands she held out to him, holding her away a little so that he might look at her. He was relieved to find no visible evidence of the agitation which had been so apparent in the letter she had penned to him with so many crossings and recrossings of lines as to make it scarcely legible.

Seeing her after an absence of several months, he was struck anew by the ease with which Kitty defied the years; absurd to reflect that she was five-and-thirty and had borne Edward three lusty children. Her figure, though a little plumper in the simple high-waisted gown which so exactly matched the blue of her eyes, still retained its girlish lines; her hair beneath that ridiculous matronly cap shone guinea bright, and there was yet about her the air of wayward innocence which had held him in thrall when, as a capricious seventeen-year-old, she had first come to London.

He and Edward, close friends from their schooldays, had very nearly come to blows that summer in their rivalry for Kitty's hand, but when she had chosen Edward, he had accepted defeat with a laconic good grace that disguised his true feelings rather better than anyone could have guessed.

It would be unrealistic to suppose that he had cherished an undying passion all these years—indeed, he had spent the better part of them demonstrating to devastating effect how heart-whole he was—but he had never found anyone who could touch his heart as that youthful Kitty had done, and in consequence he had eschewed matrimony with a determination that

3

had long been the despair of tenacious matrons with single daughters to bestow.

The slight movement of Kitty's fingers arrested his thoughts; he carried them to his lips in smiling acknowledgment of his devotion and released them.

"Oh, it is so good to see you!" Kitty exclaimed, openly admiring the superb cut of his coat fashioned of darkest olive superfine and showing a pale yellow waistcoat beneath. "Do come and sit down . . . there is so much I wish to know . . ." She drew him toward the sofa. "Did you go to Florence as you spoke of doing when you wrote from Rome? It is of all places where I should most like to go. I warn you, I shall be quizzing you forever!" As they disposed themselves comfortably she rattled on about Eliza's measles, their fears that she would not pull through, and how thin the child had grown in consequence. Gervase leaned back, amused, very much at his ease. "But the country air will soon set her up and both girls are very fond of dear Mama, and I told Edward he must stay on for as long as he wishes, Papa is sure to want to take him out shooting . . ." she met his eyes and drew breath at last on a laugh. "I am talking too much!"

Gervase protested that he was enjoying her chatter, but she shook her head and sat back, studying him afresh. He really had no business to look as he did when poor Edward was already grown quite thick around the middle—or indeed to look at one as he did—as he had always done and probably always would! It was very agreeable, of course, but unsettling in that it occasionally tempted one to hazard (disloyalty to Edward guiltily stifled) how life might have been had one chosen Gervase for a husband instead of Edward, for one would have to be a block of wood to deny his many attractions. The young gallant with the laughing, impudent eyes was no less gallant

4

now, but time and experience had refined the élan of his youth to a kind of world-weary charm tempered with cynicism—a disturbing, irresistible combination. As a lover, Gervase would be all and more than one could ever wish for. But as a husband? Ah, no . . . she had rather have dear safe, comfortable Edward for a husband any day. A little sigh of regret escaped her, nonetheless.

Gervase bore her scrutiny with the amused assurance of a man totally secure in the role he has ordained for himself. Did she, he wondered, have the least idea how expressive was her face? He shifted his position slightly in order that he might rest one arm along the back of the sofa. The movement brought her eyes to meet his. They widened a little, a tide of color and a furiously nibbled lower lip betraying the unmistakable impropriety of her thoughts. At such moments the temptation to flirt with her still assailed him; with dispassionate clarity he saw that with a very little persuasion she could be brought to respond. He put the thought firmly from him.

"You didn't mind my writing to you so soon?" she asked rather quietly.

He told her not to be goose-ish, but wondered how she had learned so promptly of his return.

"Well, Amabel Freemantle just happened to be visiting in Grosvenor Square last evening," Kitty explained, "and she saw your carriage arrive . . ."

"Ah! You need say no more!"

"Yes . . . well, you know how it is. Her maidservant told my Letty, and Letty told me . . . and I must say it did seem like an act of Providence, for I had been in such a Despair!"

Gervase was not unduly perturbed by this passionate disclosure, for Kitty's despairs were well known to him. "I think you had better tell me all," he said encouragingly. "You will feel very much more

5

the thing when you have bared your soul. Are you in some kind of scrape that you don't wish Edward to know about?"

"Good gracious . . . certainly not! I cannot imagine how you could suppose anything of the kind!" Her eyes met his highly quizzical ones and outraged virtue melted into giggles. "I daresay you are remembering that time when I pledged my beautiful sapphire collar and earrings at the loo table and you won them back for me. Edward found out and he was *so* angry!" She sighed. "What a long time ago it all seems! I don't behave foolishly anymore." She sounded half regretful.

"Poor, staid, old married lady!" Gervase teased, and before she could protest, "You don't need my compliments to tell you that you are not one whit less lovely than you were then. You have only to consult your looking glass." She blushed like a girl. "So, if you are not in trouble," he persisted gently, "why am I here?"

Kitty stared. "But you know why. It was in the letter."

"Quite possibly," he drawled. "Could I but have deciphered the contents."

"Oh." Kitty looked uncomfortable. It was one thing to pour out all her misgivings on paper, but quite another to find the right words with his sardonic eye upon her. "Well, the thing is, I wanted to . . . to ask your advice about Perry."

"Your brother?" Now that he recalled, Perry's name had figured prominently in Kitty's much-ravaged missive. Turning over in his mind the more disreputable of his own youthful indiscretions, Gervase wondered what heinous crime the silly cawker had been discovered in.

"He . . . oh, Gervase, he fancies himself in love—and with the very worst kind of woman!"

It was all he could do not to laugh aloud, but the

6

eyes she raised to him were so troubled that he only said with disarming raillery, "And what kind is that, pray?"

"She is an actress—or, to be more accurate, an opera singer!"

This time he did laugh. "Really Kitty, I am surprised at you! The boy is—what? Less than one-and-twenty. Lord save us, he will tumble in and out of love a dozen times or more before he learns discretion—and what more irresistible lure can there be for a susceptible sprig of Perry's tender years than one of the theater's little charmers?"

Kitty sprang to her feet and began to pace the room. "Yes, yes—and if that were all—if only he would be content to take this woman as his mistress until his infatuation waned, I am sure I should not regard it! But the silly boy is so bewitched that he has set her above anything so tawdry as a mere affair . . ."

"Dear me—how very quixotic of him! Almost, it persuades one to wish one were twenty again!"

"Oh, Gervase . . . don't be flippant, I beg of you! I don't know what to do! Perry comes of age in two months time and he has already confided in me that it is his most ardent desire to make this—this creature his wife. He wished me to meet her, but I refused, of course. He seemed convinced that I would be his willing ally against the family." She sounded aggrieved. "And when I endeavored to point out to him how impossible the whole situation must be, he grew decidedly miffy . . ."

"Ungrateful pup!"

In her agitation Kitty quite missed the irony in his voice. "Oh, well, I daresay he did not like being put in the wrong. Only you do see, don't you, how very urgent the matter is? Perry may do something stupid and irrevocable unless . . ." At this point her courage appeared to fail her, for Gervase too had risen and

7

was regarding her with something approaching awe. "Unless," she concluded in a rush, "a gentleman of much greater experience can be found who will . . . will engage to cut him out."

"Kitty!" His voice was deceptively gentle, "I do hope you are not suggesting what I think you are suggesting?" She gazed back at him in mute appeal. "You are, by God! Oh, no, my dear girl—what you ask is impossible! Monstrous! Not even for you will I consent to seduce Perry's opera singer from under his nose!"

"I feared you would say that." Tears trembled on her lashes. "But some way must be found and I am sure no one could accomplish the thing with greater ease than you. She is quite devastating, I'm told . . . and women of her sort are very much to your taste . . ."

"Enough!" he cried, unsure whether to laugh or be outraged. "How is it, I wonder, that the most sweetly innocent of women become utterly ruthless when their loved ones are at risk?" She said nothing. He took her by the shoulders, recognizing only too well the willful set of that stubborn little chin. "Kitty, I know Perry is your favorite brother, but this is surely carrying solicitude too far? He won't thank you for it, my dear."

"He wouldn't need to know, would he?" She blinked up at him. "And besides," she insisted, "he will thank me one day because until all this happened it had been all but settled that he was to marry the eldest Morton girl." She saw that his gray eyes were cynical and was driven to defensiveness. "I know what you are thinking, but you are quite out! There has been no constraint upon either side—truly! Why, Sally Morton and Perry have been the dearest of friends for years. They would have been betrothed officially long since but for Lady Morton's father having passed away last spring, which made her family de-

8

cide to postpone the celebrations until they were out of black gloves."

"An understandable decision in the circumstances," Gervase agreed cordially.

Kitty suspected he was being flippant again, but chose to ignore the fact.

"Yes, but now, you see, they will be expecting Perry to declare himself. And you may imagine the consequences if he decides to upturn the apple cart. Poor Mama will have a fit!"

"Not to mention poor rejected Sally," he supplied helpfully.

"Exactly so!" Kitty seized eagerly upon this further affecting picture. "And as for Papa—I daren't even hazard how he will react if he is obliged to tell Lord Morton that the union cannot take place because Perry has made a mésalliance with an opera singer!"

Gervase, having been privileged to witness the awesome spectacle of the Earl of Weare in high dudgeon, could not but sympathize.

"What is Edward's opinion in the matter? Or doesn't he know?"

Kitty, with her lip caught between even white teeth and bright color staining her cheeks, was the personification of guilt. The satirical quirk of his eyebrow told her more eloquently than words that he knew Edward did not.

"Oh well, you know Edward," she said with a nervous laugh. "He would only say that I shouldn't interfere—that hopefully Perry's infatuation will burn itself out before any lasting harm is done." Concern once more overcame her. "But suppose it is not so? Amabel Freemantle has seen them together—she took the greatest delight in telling me that she had never seen anyone so totally besotted as Perry!"

"That woman again! Is Lady Freemantle's tongue never still?" he said tersely. And then, taking Kitty by

9

the shoulders, "What a pessimist you are. Don't you know better than to heed such a tattle-box?" But Kitty would not be reassured; a stifled sob escaped her and he was lost. "Very well. I can make no promises, but you had better tell me this siren's name. You *do* know her name?"

"Of course I know it. One can hardly help but know it, for Signorina Merrilli is spoken about everywhere one goes!"

"I wasn't aware that Merrilli was in London," said Gervase with interest. And, as Kitty's eyes brightened speculatively, "No, my dear, I don't know her, but I *do* know of her. In Italy they speak of her in rhapsodies."

"It is just the same here," said Kitty crossly. "It really is quite tiresome the way her praises are sung. After all, she has done little to merit so much notice—a few appearances at provincial theaters and a private concert or two—yet already she is become the rage. She drives in the Park each afternoon, usually with Perry at her side, and every gentleman within a mile flocks to her carriage. And most of her evenings, when she has no engagement, seem to be spent in company of your Madame St. Austin . . ." She saw his eyebrow lift. ". . . or that odd Mrs. Arbuthnot . . ."

"You seem singularly well informed in spite of your avowed determination to avoid the young lady! We owe that to Amabel Freemantle, too, no doubt," he said dryly. "As for Mrs. Arbuthnot? Should I know her?"

"Oh, I hardly think she is your sort." Kitty was beginning to sound decidedly peevish.

"My sort?" he queried gently.

"Well you know what I mean. She is quite plain and not young, but is exceedingly rich. Her husband was in trade I believe—and she wears strange clothes! I fancy it is her aim to be regarded as a patroness of the arts and she is just sufficient of a character to attract attention . . ."

Gervase looked at her in some surprise, even a little sternly.

"Kitty? I had never supposed you to be high in the instep."

"I am not!" Indignation sprang up and died as quickly. "You are right, of course." She blushed with remorse. "But indeed, I don't mean to be so. In fact, I rather like Mrs. Arbuthnot . . . You won't know her, for she only came to Town at the start of the year. It is simply that I am so worried about Perry, I don't know what I am saying!"

"And without cause, my dear," he said reassuringly, "for I shall own myself very much surprised if Merrilli succumbs to a boy of Perry's relative inexperience, splendid catch though you may think him, when she will have been pursued by many a gentleman twice as wealthy and with much greater address."

"Yes, but how many, I wonder, will have offered her marriage *and* a title?" said Kitty with some shrewdness.

Gervase privately thought this to be a valid consideration, but he kept his thoughts to himself, saying only, "I will allow that to be an inducement, but if the signorina's career is flourishing as it obviously is, surely a young and jealously possessive husband is the last thing she would want?"

Kitty was not convinced, but before she could say more, the door opened to admit Sair, who announced in a carefully expressionless voice that Miss Emily Phipps had called. There was barely time for more than a rueful exchange of glances before the lady was upon them, panting from the exertion of climbing the stair, her faded prettiness hung about with several filmy shawls and the whole surmounted by an extraordinary turban of puffed gauze.

11

Her start of surprise upon seeing Gervase was a masterpiece; the incoherent protestations that she would not have *dreamed* had she but known Mr. Maxwell might be here . . . only that, of course, they had supposed him to be still abroad . . . were delivered with such conviction as to bring an involuntary twitch to his lips. Very conscious of what was expected of him, however, he bowed gallantly over her hand, told her with great amiability that she looked younger every time he saw her, and begged to be allowed the privilege of handing her to a chair.

"So kind!" The blood crept into her pale cheeks. "You are all goodness! Oh, dear . . ." One of her shawls slipped to the floor and had to be rescued, but finally Miss Emily was settled to everyone's satisfaction. She glanced about her. "You know, dear Lady Kilroy, I believe I have not seen this room since you had it refurbished. What a very pretty blue . . . and the striped chintz so exactly right. I was saying to my sister only the other day that our drawing room is grown quite shabby." A wistful note entered her voice. "I had a fancy to have it made over in shades of pink, but Hester is not convinced that it will serve . . ."

Gervase had a swift mental image of Miss Emily's severely practical elder sister amid festoons of pink draperies. He kept his countenance with an effort and dared not look at Kitty.

There followed a long and somewhat convoluted explanation of the reason for her intrusion which finally resolved itself in a tentative query as to whether Lady Kilroy would be using her box at the opera next week.

"It is to be *Figaro*, you know, with that new Italian singer who was so highly commended by both the *Times* and the *Lady's Magazine* after her appearance in Birmingham . . . indeed, the *Times* went so far as to liken her performance to that of Grassini, which is quite an accolade! Ah, Grassini! There was an artiste, to be sure!"

So lost in recollection was she, that she scarcely noticed Kitty's reactions or the rather amused interest she had aroused in Mr. Maxwell.

"In consequence, there has been such a scramble for tickets that there is nothing halfway decent to be had. We do not keep a box since poor Papa died . . . and so Hester says we must forgo the pleasure . . ." Miss Emily sighed deeply. "It does seem *such* a pity! And then it suddenly occurred to me . . . Oh, do say that you don't think me presumptuous, dear Lady Kilroy . . ."

The wistfulness of this last was such that Kitty cried instinctively. "No, indeed!" and cast a swift appealing glance at Gervase who said, "My dear Miss Emily, you could never be presumptuous. As it happens, we were this moment discussing the Signorina Merrilli. Lady Kilroy is quite as eager to see her as anyone and, in the absence of Sir Edward, I am to act as her escort."

Kitty's exclamation was hastily turned into a cough as he concluded smoothly. "I would count it an honor if you and your sister would consent to come also as my guests."

Amid incoherent expressions of gratitude from Miss Emily, Gervase rose to take his leave, not one whit discomposed by the fulminating glare directed at him by Kitty.

"I shall leave Lady Kilroy to arrange matters with you," he said with magnanimity.

At the door Kitty whispered reproachfully, "How could you!"

He smiled down at her. "You will have to see her sometime, you know."

A little later that same afternoon the fashionable

promenaders in Hyde Park were pleasantly surprised to behold Mr. Maxwell riding his spirited black stallion in at the gates as though he had never been away. At his side rode a tiny vivacious lady in a russet habit that was dashingly braided, and curved neatly into a minute waist. Her gamin features were alight beneath a mass of hennaed curls and a hat like a shako tilted itself becomingly over one eye.

"I am naturally most flattered, *chéri*," Celestine St. Austin was saying, "that you should seek me out almost the moment you return. But I ask myself why? What of the fair Eloise? I trust she is not prostrated after all your travels."

For a moment his profile was austere. "I would prefer not to discuss Eloise," he said and then looked down at her, smiling faintly. "Besides, must I have a reason to seek you out, other than a very natural impatience to see you again?"

Celestine chuckled and wagged a reproving finger under his nose. "Oh, la! Now I am truly suspicious. We have known one another too long, you and I, for me to be taken in by your flattery!" She gave an elegant little shrug. "But I do not repine. Whatever may be your motive, *chéri*, it is always agreeable to be in your company."

With mutual understanding thus established, they rode on in a spirit of harmony. Matrons passing in sedate barouches bowed and exorted their eligible daughters to sit up straight and look pleasant for there was always the remote chance . . . The fashionable impures driving their smart equipages were more openly appreciative of his return. Harriette Wilson, stopping to chat, assured him that London had been very dull without him and begged his attendance at a masked ball she and her sisters were to give the following week at the Argyle Rooms.

It soon became clear to Celestine, however, that al-

14

though Gervase replied to the various greetings with all his customary charm, his mind was occasionally elsewhere. His eyes would lift to scan approaching vehicles. Her curiosity was naturally aroused, but she was content to wait upon events. Presently they came in sight of a stationary carriage drawn up at the road's edge surrounded by an eager, jostling group of horsemen. It was a sight by now so familiar that Madame had little trouble guessing who might be at the center of the good-natured melee. An infectious trill of laughter ringing out at that moment merely provided confirmation.

The sound stirred in Gervase a memory so ephemeral, so insubstantial, that it eluded identification; a voice intriguingly accented could be heard protesting some lighthearted misunderstanding. Instinctively he checked.

Madame was not a fool. "Ah!" She nodded, comprehending. "One might have guessed." And then, philosophically, ignoring the quizzical lift of his brow, "Come, and I will introduce you."

Amusedly compliant, he followed. At their approach, heads turned—several of the young hopefuls were known to him, though he was a little surprised to see his good friend, Rupert Egerton, among their number. Another surprise was Sir Hugo Severin, a middle-aged exquisite not often to be found at the forefront of such a gathering.

It was a measure of Mr. Maxwell's popularity that a path was instantly cleared for him amid much enthusiastic back-slapping and ribald comment, all of which he endured with ironical good humor. His gaze, meanwhile, went beyond them to encompass the two occupants of the carriage. The young tulip of fashion whose features bore such a marked resemblance to Kitty's was Lord Peregrine Marlowe. He was looking smug as a cream-fed cat—and small wonder, for at his side was a vision clad in a redingote of ivory twill, closed high at the neck and trimmed with swansdown, whose every line bespoke Paris.

Upon seeing him, Perry started quite perceptibly and turned to say something to his companion. The young woman's head lifted with exquisite poise, and from beneath a sweeping hat brim wide-set jade green eyes watched him come.

Chapter 2

Gervase had the oddest sensation of déjà vu—and then, quite suddenly, everything slipped into place, the laugh, the voice . . . It must have been all of three, no, four years, ago when he had visited the tiny Teatro Filodrammatico in Milan with a friend to attend the debut of a new young singer. The opera was *Le Nozze di Figaro* and the very young girl in the role of Cherubino had conquered the boisterous Italian audience with the purity of her voice, and a joyful audacity which more than compensated for her lack of expertise.

True, the young lady before him now was far removed from the pert Cherubino of his memory, for time had honed the mischievous pointed face with its overgenerous mouth into a thing of beauty, yet there was no mistaking that the two were one and the same.

Signorina Marissa Merrilli's delightful voice held a hint of gentle mockery as she extended to him a slender gloved hand, and her smile, though brilliant, held a certain wariness in its depths.

"Mr. Maxwell. I have heard much of you. It would seem that London is not fashionable where you are not!"

Gervase had brought his mount very close alongside the carriage. With ostentatious deliberation he carried her hand to his lips, retaining his hold of it a shade longer than politeness demanded.

17

"So they tell me, signorina," he agreed, mockery answering mockery, rejoicing in the challenge. "But you and I need not regard such absurdities. London"—his glance flicked over the group gathered about her—"seems to go on very well without me, wouldn't you say?"

Faint color dusted the high cheekbones, but Lord Peregrine was already claiming his attention with a brazen assurance borne of unease. "Gervase! I'd no idea you were back," he said airily. "I expect you will already have called in at Hill Street?"

"My dear boy! Do give me a chance. I only arrived in Grosvenor Square last evening. Why? Is there something I should know?"

The eagerness of Perry's denial made his relief all too apparent, but Gervase did not pursue the matter, putting up his glass instead to inspect the younger man's waistcoat. The garment was of a new and startlingly lurid design and, viewed together with the accompanying confection which adorned his neck, made him feel sadly staid. Not wishing to give offense, however, he allowed his glass to fall without comment.

Perry grinned, unabashed. "I daresay you won't care for it, but it's all the crack!"

"Then I am well served for remaining so long abroad," murmured Gervase equivocally.

"No! I say, dash it all . . ." An amiable argument ensued among those listening, during which the signorina laid a quiet reassuring hand upon Perry's coat sleeve. He at once covered it eagerly with one of his own.

The significance of that small intimacy was not lost upon Gervase. So, he mused, the lady had her victim very neatly ensnared. Her intentions might well be pure, but one thing was immediately evident—if she chose to spring the trap, Perry would be a most willing prey. In spite of all his firmly avowed intentions, interest began to stir as the signorina came quickly to Perry's defense.

"I think Lord Marlow looks very dashing."

"Do you, indeed?" said Gervase with sardonic amusement.

"Yes, Mr. Maxwell, I do." She leaned forward, a fluid movement which displayed to perfection the supple grace of her figure. "Youth is the time for experiment, as I am sure you must agree." She gave him a long, considering look, head back and a little to one side. The full, brooding lower lip took a delicious upward curve as she smiled challengingly into his eyes. "Of course, one can appreciate that it would not do for you!"

"Pinked, by Jove!" chortled Perry.

Gervase saluted the lady's quickness without the least loss of humor, but resolved that in his own good time he would exact payment for her impertinence. He moved away a little and found Sir Hugo Severin's thin drawl insistent in his ear.

"Our little diva reveals herself in a new guise—not only is she beautiful and talented, but is also a wit, perforce!"

Major Rupert Egerton, late of the Ninety-fifth Rifles, riding across to greet Gervase, was in time to hear this malicious observation. His normally mild, good-humored manner became stiffly formal as he nodded briefly toward the middle-aged dandy for whom he had little time. Then he reached forward to grasp Gervase by the hand.

"My dear fellow, how are you? Good to have you back—or are you weary of people saying that?"

"That would be churlish of me indeed." Gervase smiled at his stocky friend. Rupert grinned back, jerking his head toward Severin who had swung his mount around and resumed his place beside the carriage.

"He lusts after the lady, of course. He will not love you should you resolve to cut him out."

"Then surely it is Perry who must incur his wrath," Gervase protested mildly. "I scarcely know the signorina."

"Such masterly indifference might fool a lesser man, dear old fellow, but I've seen that *measuring* look in your eye too often!" The major's mobile mouth quirked irrepressibly. "It bears the indisputable hallmark of the hunter sizing up his prey!"

Marissa, too, recognized that look. She had encountered it many times. It was the look his kind of man reserved exclusively for her kind of woman and coming to terms with it had been one of the hardest disciplines she had been obliged to learn. Yet this time there was a subtle difference; in that first moment of meeting she had felt the peculiar little shiver along her nerves which came only at rare and special moments. And ever since, while she laughed and flirted and cajoled, her mind had been in a turmoil.

It was ridiculous, even a little frightening, that the cool insolence of those dark eyes could affect her so profoundly; she had even the oddest notion that he had seen right through her in a way that no one else had ever done. It had taken every ounce of assurance she possessed to appear unconcerned.

Irresistibly her glance strayed to where he sat now, astride his raking black hunter with so much ease, conversing with Major Egerton—infernally attractive, infernally assured! As though aware of her surging confusion, he turned to regard her with a curious intensity, and the color, stealing into her cheeks, betrayed her.

Oh, this would not do! She said with defiant gaiety: "Gentlemen, you are too kind, but I must leave you now. No, truly—" She put up a hand to stay their concerted protest. "I have a singing lesson in a very few minutes, and if I am late I shall be in disgrace with my dear Signor Pucci who is most strict in such matters. Until we meet tonight, my friends." She nodded to Perry, who gave her coachman the office to start. As they drew level with Mr. Maxwell, she bade him farewell, bestowing upon him her most brilliant smile.

"Arrividerci, signorina." He bowed with exaggerated deference. "Servant, Perry."

There was a small silence as they drove toward the Park gates. Then Marissa said casually, "This Mr. Maxwell—he has an air about him. Do you know him well?"

"Lord, yes," Perry replied. "Been around for as long as I can remember. He and Sir Edward Kilroy . . . my sister Kitty's husband . . . are friends of very long standing."

"And you like him?"

"Oh, most people like Gervase! He's so deucedly amiable, it's difficult to do otherwise . . . and, of course, it goes without saying that females almost always fall victim to that dilettante charm!" Perry sounded vaguely envious. "Kitty dotes on him! That's why I wondered . . ."

"Yes?" He failed to notice the odd note in her voice.

"I daresay it's nothing, but . . . well, I've sometimes thought that Gervase might cherish a tendre for Kitty and it did occur to me when he came upon us like that so soon after his return, that she might have . . ." He shrugged the unwelcome thought away and finished somewhat ambiguously, "But I shouldn't think it likely for, even if she did, *he* wouldn't. It ain't his way."

Marissa did not pursue the matter; she did not need explanations, for much was suddenly clear to her. "Mr. Maxwell is very rich, I suppose?"

21

"As a nabob, I shouldn't wonder!" Perry moved irritably. "I say, do we have to talk about Gervase?"

"No, of course not." She caught guiltily at her lip. She had no intention of succumbing to Mr. Maxwell's much-vaunted charm.

Perry must have been thinking along similar lines. "Sometimes I wish you weren't so . . . so deucedly in demand!" he blurted out. "I can almost never be alone with you."

"You are alone with me now," she teased, willing him not to be tiresome.

"That is not what I mean!" He grasped her hand eagerly. "Marissa, do we have to go to this affair of Mrs. Arbuthnot's this evening?"

"Of course we must go. This lady has been most kind to me . . . it would be ungrateful to the extreme to spurn her invitation!"

"I suppose so. It was just a thought . . . Then can I come and sit with you while you have your singing lesson?" he pleaded. "I promise faithfully that I won't make a sound!"

"Oh no!" Her laugh rose on the air. "No, Perry. That would not be a good idea!" He looked so crestfallen that she explained more kindly, "Cosmo, you see, would not care for it. He wishes the whole of my concentration."

"Then take this now and say you will wear it tonight!" Perry fumbled eagerly in his pocket and drew out a small enamel box with gilded corners. Inside the box nestled a beautiful pearl-set brooch.

"My dear, you shouldn't!" she protested, smoothing the delicate translucent object with one gentle fingertip. "You give me too many presents already!"

"Not half as many as I *would* give you, if you'd only say the word! I would shower you with jewels . . . and one in particular . . ."

"Oh, Perry, not now—you promised!" Marissa was

beginning to feel trapped; with a feeling of profound relief she saw they were turning the corner into Arlington Street. "Come now," she urged as he looked mulishly set to argue, "I have already explained. Signor Pucci has worked so hard for me, and with me; he has recently been very ill! How can I contemplate a marriage that will wreck all his hopes for me just when they are being fulfilled?"

"You could continue with your singing . . ." he muttered.

"That wouldn't work, you know it wouldn't." She gathered up her reticule and her parasol as the carriage drew to a halt. "Perry, I must go in" She hesitated over the brooch, but he folded it into her hand and pressed his lips to it fervently before rushing to help her down. On the pavement she lifted her free hand to touch his cheek. "I will see you tonight, yes? Do not be unhappy, *caro*. There is much time for both of us, after all. Let us enjoy what we have. Pietro." She addressed her coachman. "Take Lord Marlowe where he wishes to go."

"No. I will walk," Perry said and walked quickly away.

It had been a strange afternoon, full of unsettling portents. Marissa drifted up the curving staircase, trailing the plume of her beautiful hat, filled with a vague, not wholly unpleasing melancholia. Would that one might be delivered from dedication and obligation and become as a butterfly, a free-as-air uncommitted Society butterfly, lighting as and where one pleased, such as those women for whom she so often performed. Were they content, she wondered, with a life given over solely to the pursuit of pleasure?

But if to be indulged was what she craved, there had been offers enough in all conscience—undeniably handsome offers, from great and important men.

"You are a fool!" one of her fellow artistes had once

sneered, driven no doubt by jealousy when Marissa repulsed the lecherous Grand Duke Ludwig of Saxe-Coberg for the second time. "Do not suppose for one moment that anyone truly believes you to be virtuous! Would that any of us could afford the luxury—nay, the sheer folly—of being able to spurn such patronage!"

Marissa sighed. Was it folly to crave respectability? If so, then it must be folly to allow Perry so much license! If only he were not so young, so intense! She didn't know whether the idiotic reverence in which he held her should be a cause for laughter or tears—she only knew that the sheer novelty of it entranced her. It was madness indeed not to marry him out of hand before his passion began to wane, but that would be poor recompense for one who paid her so signal an honor.

And now Mr. Maxwell had come along, intent upon preventing the match! She knew it as surely as if he had said so.

At this point Marissa's reverie was shattered; a shadow of immense proportions filled the doorway of a room on the upper landing, revealed itself as female, and flowed toward her enveloped in a quantity of lilac twill and surmounted by a splendid beribboned cap.

"Maria of the Skies!" intoned a voice whose resonance a basso profundo would not have disowned. The hat was twitched from Marissa's unresisting fingers, lifted to the light and lovingly tended. "Is this the way to treat such a plume? I tell you, we have servants to sweep the stair"—a scornful glance defied the truth of this assertion—"though who would ever presume it to behold the dirt!"

"I'm sorry, Tia Giannina," said Marissa meekly. "I didn't think."

"But naturally! Why should you think when there are closets filled with all manner of bonnets and fripperies to choose?" The voice followed Marissa with remorseless energy into the white and gold bedchamber, the ample figure successfully negotiating the spiraling columns of a canopied bed to swoop with marvelous agility upon the already carelessly discarded redingote, deftly folding it and in the same movement, it seemed, handing her charge into a silk-flounced wrapper which tied becomingly beneath the bosom.

"Who would believe now the child that came to us seven years ago in her skimpy muslin dress, the eyes filling that thin little face? Fifteen years you were, as God is witness, and with the body of a boy, so nearly did the bones come through your skin! How many bowls of Tia Giannina's fine steaming golden polenta did it take to make of you a young woman! And you are still too thin!" The signora spoke with all the complacence of one who has curves, and to spare.

She whisked her unprotesting charge across to the dressing mirror, deposited her on the stool before it and, removing the pins, began vigorously to brush out the sable hair that came rippling down until it shone.

Signora Tortinallo had been housekeeper to Signor Pucci for more than forty years. For most of those years life had been agreeably uneventful with only the occasional flat arpeggio from an aspiring pupil, the occasional outburst of hysteria, to disrupt the harmony in the gracious little Venetian palazzo on one of the quiet campos away from the bustle of the Grand Canal. Sometimes indeed the maestro would be away for months at a time, traveling the great cities of the world with one of his protégés, and then there was a wealth of time to be filled.

But all had changed on the day Signor Pucci had

returned, bringing with him the daughter of his cousin Rosa—God rest her—who had herself been a diva of great promise in the days before a feckless charming husband had carried her away to Dublin and a life entirely wretched. The signora had taken one look and without a moment's thought had enlarged her duties with careless magnanimity to embrace into her charge the shy, grave-eyed girl who spoke Italian like an Italian and had inherited all of her mother's talent.

In an instant she was no longer a mere housekeeper but Tia Giannina (an incongruous-sounding appellation for one built on such generous lines), dear friend, instructress and—when the maestro had deemed Marissa ready to display her talents before a waiting world—she had become dresser, eagle-eyed chaperone and factotum, though nowadays her duties as chaperone were spurned, and more was the pity, thought the signora with a sniff.

"Come," she instructed, threading a ribbon swiftly through Marissa's hair. "The Maestro has waited long enough—ten minutes ago his brows were *so*—" The signora's own superb eyebrows met across her nose in graphic illustration.

Marissa's Italian love of the dramatic which served her so well in Opera vied with her Irish sense of humor. She struck an attitude. "Then all is lost!" she cried tragically, one limp wrist pressed to her forehead.

The frown deepened.

With a gurgle of laughter that Gervase would have recognized instantly, Marissa sprang up with a placating gesture. "Very well. Behold. I am already gone!"

She entered the drawing room quietly and closed the door, standing with her back to it.

Signor Pucci occupied a wing chair near the fireplace, one painfully thin, yet graceful hand extended to the comforting blaze. It was immediately obvious that Tia Giannina had been less than truthful; there was no frown marring the fine wide brow; indeed in all the time Marissa had known him she had never seen Cosmo Pucci display open anger. In displeasure he simply went away from one, and became as a stranger, an experience so chilling to the soul that one did not take undue liberties. For the most part, however, though he demanded only the very best of one, he was infinitely patient, infinitely kind.

He looked across at Marissa now, his eyes very much alive in a face pared almost to the bone by illness; the hair grown snow-white. Yet his figure was still erect, his dress impeccable. A smile touched lips that were faintly tinged with blue.

"You present a delightful picture of demure innocence standing there, my dear. No doubt you hope it will blind me to the fact that you are ten minutes late?"

"I'm sorry." She abandoned her pose with a quick beguiling grin and crossed the room swiftly to crouch at his knee. "It was one of those afternoons, you know? The time just . . . went!"

"I comprehend perfectly," he said dryly. "It is very agreeable to be made much of, is it not?" The pause was infinitesimal. "So long as you do not forget what is the true purpose of your visit."

It was almost a reprimand. Marissa recognized it as such and knew it to be justified. The knowledge instantly dispelled the small surge of rebellion that rose in her—he had been so good, and her London debut, she knew, meant so much to him.

"I won't let you down, Cosmo," she said abruptly.

"Of course you will not." His fingers stroked her cheek lightly. "Come, we will say no more about it. There is work to be done."

Cosmo Pucci's equable demeanor remained unaltered, showing nothing of that great hollow of fear which gripped him whenever he contemplated the future. He was not a fool; the doctors made reassuring noises, though they had thrown up their hands at this present visit—"to leave Italy for the fogs and mists of London at this time, signor, is a madness!" But he knew that the hours of his days were numbered, and he feared that time would run out before he had done for Marissa all that he had set himself to do. Occasionally he even questioned whether he had done her a service in taking her from the safe obscurity of her Irish background, but that doubt never troubled him for long. Marissa, through a closeness to her mother, was in many ways more Italian than Irish—and to have deprived her of the chance to develop her talent would have been a crime, as events had since proved.

But it was not sufficient to establish her as a diva of international repute. He desperately wanted to be assured that she would also be cared for in the way that he cared for her. There were many, he knew, who cynically misinterpreted the nature of his relationship with Marissa. He had not actively discouraged the calumny, for at least it afforded Marissa a degree of protection. There had been admirers, of course—lighthearted flirtations, for the most part, a proposition here and there as was inevitable, but she had dealt kindly with them all. Yet he knew that she had inherited her mother's passionate nature—his Rosa whom he had loved more irrevocably than either of them could ever have guessed. One day that passion would waken.

He lived in dread that some unscrupulous man would come along who would use Marissa, or, almost as bad, that she would throw away her life on someone totally ineffectual as had her mother. This Lord

Marlowe, for instance—little more than a boy. True, she had laughingly dismissed any thought of taking him seriously, but still—a union of such respectability could present a temptation, and would be a disaster!

Chapter 3

The first glimpse of Mrs. Arbuthnot's Palladian villa situated near the river at Chiswick promised an eccentricity to delight the soul. The shallow balustraded semicircle of steps leading to the open front door was illuminated by six blazing flambeaux borne aloft by six motionless footmen wearing Turkish trousers.

As a hostess Mrs. Arbuthnot was so far removed from the usual image of the *haut ton* matron that her social evenings were invariably crowded, with young people mostly, for she liked to have young people about her—and they, for their part, found her oddity and the complete absence of any kind of formality a refreshing and novel experience.

"We don't stand on ceremony here," she told Gervase as he apologized for arriving uninvited. The clipped voice which betrayed her northern origins sounded wholly incongruous, coming as it did from this quick, slight apparition clad in the most extraordinary Oriental robe worn with casual aplomb over a pair of flame-red harem trousers. Short dark hair without the vestige of a kink framed an ageless face; restless eyes probed his face with interest, noted the long sensitive mouth which showed an agreeable tendency to quirk upward, measured the cut of his black evening coat, and dwelt for a speculative moment upon the diamond pin winking among the folds of his cravat.

When her eyes lifted again to meet his amused

ones, she was not one whit discomposed, but gave a brisk little nod of approval. "Celestine did quite right to bring you. I trust you will have a pleasant evening." An arm festooned with gold bracelets jangled in a delightfully vague gesture of dismissal as she turned to greet the next of her guests.

Gervase would not have missed any of it for the world. "Is there a Mr. Arbuthnot?"

"Not for many years. He was, so far as one can discover, something in the manufacturing way and had already amassed an immense fortune before ever Matilda was coerced into marriage with him by her father."

"She does not appear to me to be a lady who would coerce easily," Gervase said.

"There were strong family pressures put upon her, I believe. Perhaps she decided that Mr. Arbuthnot would be the lesser of two evils! And in the event he did not very long survive the marriage."

"Worn down, perhaps, by all that nervous energy!"

Celestine grinned. "It would be idle to pretend that she had much affection for her husband. She once confided to me that he was such a dreadful nip-farthing that it has given her the greatest pleasure to be outrageously extravagant with his money! Also she provides for his workers far more generously than he ever did—and devotes much time to good works."

"And travels widely, I believe you told me."

"Prodigiously!"

The salon into which they were presently shown resembled more nearly than anything else, a sultan's seraglio. Its high-domed ceiling was entirely worked in mosaic lavishly embellished with gold, from which hung lamps in exquisitely wrought holders. The walls depicted, in a series of paneled frescoes, scenes of entwined lovers in a complexity of attitudes, some inno-

31

cent and some, Gervase was moved to observe dryly, which if fully comprehended, would be guaranteed to send any gently nurtured lady or gentlemen tottering in search of the hartshorn.

"When may we expect the houris to appear?" he murmured wickedly.

Rupert, who had joined them, laughed. "A bit of a facer, ain't it?"

"Each room depicts a country which Matilda has particularly enjoyed visiting," Celestine explained. "It gives one to pause, does it not?"

"It does, indeed!"

A small commotion near the door heralded the arrival of Signorina Merrilli with her inevitable entourage. She stood for a moment supremely confident as though on stage, inviting adulation. A dress of soft green silk draped low at the neck was cunningly bound about her figure by a golden cord so that it clung with Grecian simplicity to her slim curves. Her hair was gathered high on a head proudly held.

Gervase caught her eye and bowed in mock homage; she acknowledged his salutation with a gracious nod. Then she was surrounded once more and carried forward with the crowd.

As they passed close he heard Perry say with youthful urgency, "When we are married I shall not permit you to be importuned! You shall perform only as and when you please!"

A gurgle of laughter greeted this impassioned declaration, and as her voice faded away, "Oh, when we are *married*, my lord . . ."

When next he caught a glimpse of her, she was reclining upon a sofa in a far corner, holding court. She was in the highest good humor—and small wonder for it seemed at a brief glance that every young gallant in the room was either draped over the high-backed sofa or lay at her feet, each carefully disordered coiffure resting upon the striped satin upholstery as close to their Divinity as propriety would allow, and the closest of all was Perry.

As the evening progressed, a plentiful supply of iced champagne insured a merry mood. Soon, many of the young people were dancing, waltzing with an air of abandon that would have been much frowned upon by the august patronesses of Almack's. It seemed that Marissa was never off her feet for more than a few minutes at a time.

"Such energy!" sighed Celestine as they met briefly between times. "Would that I had so much!"

Marissa wrinkled her nose and said casually, looking across to the far corner, "Mr. Maxwell dances very little."

"Ah, but then he considers himself beyond all this frivolity! Which is but a pose, for if he truly wished, he could waltz us all off our feet!"

The same thought had occurred to Marissa the very first time she had seen him across the room, slim-hipped and with the lithe, springing stride which denotes the good dancer. She was astonished to discover how much she wanted to waltz with him—it must be the champagne which filled her with such reckless thoughts. She had taken only a very little for Cosmo was very strict about such things when she was so close to a performance. Nor did he care to have her sing too often and without discrimination. Yet it was impossible that she should refuse when, presently, the demand for a song was quickly taken up around the room. She was carried amid laughing protests and lifted onto a dais much ornamented with flowers and greenery where the musicians already waited.

She stood for a moment gazing down at them all, irresolute; then, with a graceful fatalistic gesture, she

33

turned to consult the musicians' leader. A spontaneous cheer arose.

"Three short songs only, my friends," she pleaded charmingly. "Even for this much Signor Pucci would scold me severely, were he here. He wishes me to conserve my voice."

She saw that Mr. Maxwell had moved forward so that he was close to the dais, but the moment she commenced to sing, all else was forgotten.

Her voice had lost none of the purity Gervase remembered—rather it had deepened and matured quite beyond his expectations. She had chosen her brief repertoire well—"Cherry Ripe," delivered with a fine sense of pace and gaiety, was followed by a winsome little ballad which evoked many a sigh, and to finish, a passionate Italian love song which left her audience enraptured and shouting for more.

But to all cries of "Encore" she shook her head, standing quite still, eyes shining, her hands clasped simply before her like a child. In that moment, while no one moved, Gervase stepped forward, applauding with the rest.

"Bravo, *cara mia*," he said softly, looking up into her eyes. She made no attempt to move, indeed, she was not sure that she *could* move for there was something in that look which made her feel exposed as she had never felt on stage—and foolish! She discovered that her legs were trembling and her tongue had cleaved to the roof of her mouth for all the world as though she were some gauche schoolroom miss.

And then, as though aware of her predicament, his eyes crinkled into gentle laughter.

"Permit me," he said and before she knew it his hands had encircled her and she was lifted effortlessly to the ground. For an interminable moment he held her, while his gray eyes smiled down into hers with a disturbing vibrance in their depths; his thumbs rested lightly just below the curve of her breasts so that he could hardly fail to notice how her heart was jolting against her ribs. And still she could not speak.

It was Charlie Hallam who broke the spell, his bluff genial voice booming out. "Maxwell, dear fellow, do put our little prima donna down. Burn it—not five minutes home and you're already at your tricks! Might at least have the decency to wait for a proper introduction!"

Perry was by now at Marissa's side, possessive, trying hard to swallow a quite allowable indignation. And suddenly, everyone was crowding around.

Gervase released Marissa, his eyes still laughing at her, and at last she felt a healthy little spurt of anger. In a clear, amused voice she said, "Oh but we *did* meet this afternoon, Mr. Hallam—very briefly, though I suspect Mr. Maxwell would have behaved in exactly the same fashion without benefit of introduction!"

"So he would, my love," gurgled Celestine. "How clever of you to know it!"

Marissa threaded her arm through Perry's and laughed over her shoulder as she left. "Ah, but then in the theater one learns very quickly to assess character."

On the fringe of the group Sir Hugo Severin watched, his handsome, rather florid features expressionless. At his side a stylish lady of middle years tittered archly. "Mr. Maxwell wastes no time, I see. He is constantly astonishing one, is he not? Who would have supposed that he would tire of Eloise Marchant so soon! Though to have abandoned her in Rome is not quite what one expects of him for he is, in general, a generous-natured man." Lady Freemantle was well launched into her peroration. Her voice dropped discreetly, but not before she was comfortably aware that her audience had grown. "One must suppose he had his reasons. But Eloise! So very beautiful, you know, and his taste is always so . . . exquisite! One wondered where his eye would light next. Now, perhaps, we need look no further!" She ended with a coy laugh, and as an after-thought, "Poor Perry!"

Sir Hugo had turned his head slowly to look at her, his mouth turned thinly downward in disbelief. "Your pardon, ma'am, am I to understand that the affair between Mr. Maxwell and Eloise Marchant is at an end?"

"Oh, yes. Quite, quite at an end!" She was all wide-eyed innocence. "Dear me! Have I been indiscreet?"

Like a light set to dry kindling the rumor spread through the room until it reached the group near the dais.

"Is it true?" Celestine asked, much intrigued.

"That I left Eloise in Rome?" Gervase looked across the heads of those nearest to him and caught a glimpse of Lady Freemantle's brassy blond curls, a plump rouged cheek; at that moment he would cheerfully have throttled her with the rope of pearls wound about that plumply pretty, ever inquisitive neck. "Yes, it is true," he admitted, a small frown disturbing his brow. "But I don't believe you can expect me to elaborate."

Rupert, however, was not content to let the matter lie. The evening being warm, he, like the rest, had partaken liberally of Mrs. Arbuthnot's excellent champagne and was now in rollicking good humor.

"Burn it, Gervase, you can't leave us all up in the air!" he cried. "You're among friends, after all. That little bud of promise bleed you, did she?" he hazarded with a knowing leer. "I thought she would!"

"Rupert, you really must not tempt me to be ungallant . . ."

"No, that wouldn't do it," Charlie Hallam cut in

with the devastating logic of the inebriate. "Maxwell ain't mean, whatever else he may be. It's my belief the little charmer tried to cozen him into marrying her."

There was a small uncomfortable silence during which Celestine's finely plucked brows almost vanished into her vastly becoming fringe of red-gold curls and Mr. Maxwell took snuff from a tiny enameled box with a curious air of abstraction. It was a silence that no one seemed willing to break.

"Come," said Celestine at last, linking one arm through his and one through Rupert's. "We will all take a little stroll in the gardens before supper."

"A tactful exit, my dear? I think not," said Gervase, gently loosing her hold of him. "To leave matters as they now stand would give rise to all kinds of speculation, whereas the truth is much more commonplace and don't reflect half so well on me." His eyes traveling around the group were faintly mocking. "The truth being that whilst in Rome I introduced Eloise to an Austrian count—a passing acquaintance—who repayed me by stealing her from under my very nose. One could hardly blame her—the prospect of becoming his countess! By now she will be installed in Vienna!"

There was some sympathetic laughter into which Mrs. Arbuthnot said calmly, "Well, I hadn't the pleasure of knowing the young lady, but I'd say she'd done rather better for herself than she deserved."

Gervase regarded his hostess with renewed interest, and decided that she would repay a closer acquaintance.

"And now," she said. "I think we'll all take supper."

"Sorry about that, dear old fellow," said Rupert sheepishly as they made their way into an adjoining salon. "A bit foxed, y'know."

"Forget it. The story had to come out sooner or later."

"No one, of course, believes that there is not a lot more to it," Celestine murmured wickedly, "but it will suffice." Curiosity impelled her to add, "Did Eloise really marry this count?"

"She did." A glint came into his eye. "But it was not achieved without a great deal of scheming on my part!"

They all laughed and turned their attention to the supper tables laid out with all manner of delicacies interspersed every so often with exquisite baskets, fashioned of gold lattice work, filled to overflowing with peaches and pineapples and fat black grapes. Rupert began happily to pile a plate high with lobster patties and quail eggs in aspic and several cuts of meat.

Marissa meanwhile ate very little. Beside her Sir Hugo was delivering a cuttingly witty account of what had just passed to the rest of the table, aided and abetted by Mr. Hallam who, every now and then, turned to a pretty blond child who knelt on the chair beside him feeding grapes into his upturned mouth. It occurred to Marissa suddenly that Sir Hugo had little love for Mr. Maxwell. It was left to Perry to champion him, though even he laughed as heartily as the rest.

"To be fair," he said, "Gervase has never made any secret of his views on marriage ..."

"Aye. Well, why should he don leg shackles when he's never lacked for beautiful women to warm his bed ... Oh, y're pardon, signorina." Charlie Hallam had the grace to look embarrassed.

"Do not trouble about me, signor," she said politely.

"Are you all right, Marissa?" whispered Perry, finding her unaccountably quiet. "Is all this a bit much for you?" His solicitude irked her.

38

"No, no. A slight headache. It will pass," she said. Across the room Mr. Maxwell bit into a pasty and seemed not the least bit perturbed by the possibility that he was being discussed on all sides. Celestine said something to him and he put back his head and laughed. No doubt with so many conquests to his credit he took little account of gossip. It was stupid, perhaps, to let the talk about Mr. Maxwell's mistress affect her; but did men, she wondered, discuss her in a similar fashion when she was not there to hear them? Did they, these charming elegant men, assess her good points, her potential, her availability? The lights blurred and danced before her eyes . . .

She rose rather abruptly from her chair, laid a restraining hand on Perry's arm when he would have risen too, and dismissed all expressions of concern. Only after a brief, impatient exchange of words, however, was Perry dissuaded from accompanying her from the room.

Gervase was intrigued. He had been observing Marissa while Rupert regaled him with the latest on dits about Prinny and his tiresome wife; had noted that although her posture was inherently graceful, there was just a hint of a droop to the shoulders draped so becomingly in soft green silk. Several times she had pressed her fingers surreptitiously to her temples as though the crowning profusion of her sable hair had suddenly grown too heavy for her slender neck.

He waited until he thought his own departure would pass unnoticed before making his excuses. And had almost reached the door when a piercing voice that could not be ignored called his name. He turned to face Lady Freemantle, concealing his exasperation behind a blank wall of politeness.

"Mr. Maxwell . . . I simply had to speak to you!" she gushed. "I am so terribly afraid that a tiny in-

39

discretion of mine might have been the cause of some embarrassment to you!"

Gervase bowed, his eyes ruthlessly assessing the pretty, empty face, expertly painted to give the illusion that she was still young, and he thought of Kitty who had no need of any such aids.

"Pray do not distress yourself unnecessarily, ma'am," he said with crushing formality. "Heaven forfend that anyone should accuse *you* of being indiscreet!"

"I am pleased to hear you say so," she replied in all seriousness. "For you have but to hear how it came about and you will see how the misunderstanding arose. I just happened to see you returning home quite alone..."

"But I was not alone, ma'am." Impatience made Gervase sharp with her.

"You were not?" Her pale blue eyes grew round with the awful possibility that something had escaped her prurient gaze.

"Certainly not," he concluded. "I was accompanied as ever by my faithful valet Dobson."

He bowed again and left her before she had time to draw breath.

By the time he reached the wide semicircular gallery which ran around the head of the staircase, it was empty except for the flunkies positioned at intervals like statues. The doors leading from it were all closed. Cursing Amabel Freemantle heartily, he strolled along and stopped in front of the first footman.

"A young lady came this way?" he inquired pleasantly.

The man hesitated. Gervase took a coin from his pocket and flipped it casually under the flunkey's nose. "Would you blight the course of true love?" he murmured persuasively.

40

The man watched the spiraling shimmer of gold with covetous eyes; the woman had been quite urgent in her plea for privacy, but who was he, after all, to fathom the odd quirks of women or the gentry that pursued them? He jerked his head abruptly in the direction of the nearest door.

"My thanks," said Gervase softly. He spun the coin once more and the man caught it neat as ninepence.

The door was not properly latched. Gervase pushed it open upon a small anteroom and saw Marissa framed in the soft light shed by twin candelabra placed at either side of the fireplace. She was standing at an oval table, head bent, her hands braced palms downward on the table top, her graceful body arched.

He shut the door quietly, but not quietly enough; without looking up, she said on an edgy kind of sob, "Oh *Dio*, Perry! Do please go away! I just want to be alone for a while."

"How very unsociable!" Gervase murmured. "But I know exactly how you must feel. That boy's solicitude would be decidedly wearing if one wasn't feeling quite the thing."

Marissa straightened up with an obvious effort and turned to face him. Her eyes seemed to be drowning in deep shadow. "Mr. Maxwell, am I to be singled out yet again?" She drew an unsteady breath. "I daresay you have been used to thinking that all women find you irresistible, but I beg you to believe that it is not so with me!"

"Are you sure?" There was a hint of a laugh in his voice. "A little while ago I could have sworn it was quite otherwise! But, no matter. I am really quite harmless, you know. In fact, I am generally thought to be the most amiable of men. If I have led you to think otherwise, then you must allow me to make

41

amends." He saw her sway slightly and abandoned his teasing. With his most charming smile he drew a chair forward. "Please, do sit down."

"I am sorry . . ." She frowned at him dully as though she had difficulty understanding his purpose. "In other circumstances I might feel better able to humor you, but at this present time I am in no mood to play your games."

"Of course you are not," he said soothingly. "But you misunderstand me."

"Do I?" Her voice, breaking on an abrupt laugh, had acquired a huskiness that was oddly endearing. She drew herself up very straight, pride in every line. "Mr. Maxwell, I think you should know here and now that I have not the least intention of becoming your next inamorata."

His eyebrow described a wildly quizzical arch. "Signorina," he said gently, "you have not been asked!"

"Oh!" She bit her lip in vexatious confusion, and though the candlelight was kind, he knew that she blushed. "Then ... I don't see ..."

"You have the migraine, I believe?" He did not wait for answer. "Well, I have come to offer you, not a cure, perhaps, but at least a little relief."

"Are you then a miracle worker?" she said grudgingly.

"No. But I do have a certain talent—if you will permit?" He indicated the chair.

"Thank you," she said too quickly, reaching for her reticule and fumbling inside. "You are very kind, but I do have my own remedy ..."

Gervase took the small vial from her trembling fingers, removed the stopper briefly to sniff it, and glanced up to regard her with a fleeting frown. "Laudanum?"

"A few drops, only," she said defensively. "And I seldom have need of it."

"Well, you certainly won't need any tonight." He replaced the vial in her reticule. Marissa endeavored to retrieve it in a gesture of sheer panic and found her hand caught and held. With his other hand he tipped her head up until her eyes, narrowed with pain, met his. "Are you afraid of me?" he said softly.

She moved her head negatively; even so slight a movement made her wince. "I . . . scarcely know you."

He smiled. "Oh, I think you do. I think we understand one another rather well! But all that can come later, so do stop being difficult, dear girl. I promise that for now you have nothing to fear."

Marissa sighed and surrendered herself to this persuasive, unpredictable man. She offered no more than a token resistance as he helped her to the chair.

"No, not like that. Sit back and try to relax—that's the way of it. Now, close your eyes."

His first touch sent a faint tremor through her, but his voice was quietly reassuring and soon his fingers were moving surely across her shoulders, a steady circular rhythm carrying them right up into the nape of her neck. The effect was at once both sensual and soothing and any lingering will to resist left her as the pain began to melt away . . .

Gervase was more disturbed by Marissa's nearness than he had expected to be. The softness of her skin was warm to his touch, like silk; her hair, sheened by the candlelight, exuded a faint tantalizing fragrance which made him long to bring it tumbling down so that he might bury his face in it.

She really had no business to have surrendered herself quite so completely to his ministrations. There was a terrible trusting vulnerability about that serene

43

profile, now freed from the shadow of pain, which reproached him; at such a moment as this one might almost be tempted to believe, as Perry so plainly did, that she was an untouched innocent. It was an assumption as unsettling as it was unlikely. Perhaps, after all, it would be a kindness to Perry to take her away from him.

His fingers stilled. With quiet deliberation he removed them and stood aside.

"That should do, I think," he said. "How do you feel?"

"Wonderful!" Marissa's eyelids fluttered reluctantly and lifted; she stared up at him with dark languorous eyes, until something in his expression prodded her into full consciousness; she sat up rather quickly and regretted it. "Well, perhaps wonderful is overstating it a little," she added, catching her breath on an enchanting half-embarrassed giggle, "but I am exceedingly grateful to you, nonetheless."

A sudden burst of laughter came from somewhere beyond the door, disturbing the quietness of the room briefly. She said diffidently, "Mr. Maxwell, I wonder—would you do me the further kindness of finding Mrs. Arbuthnot for me so that I may make my apologies . . . and perhaps, if it is not too great an imposition . . . arrange for my carriage to be brought round? I don't think I can face all those people again tonight."

"I am yours to command, signorina," he said lightly. "And Perry?"

"Oh, *Dio!*" She looked slightly harassed. "Would it be too awful if I abandoned him here? He will make a great fuss of me and I do not think . . ."

It needed but a moment for Gervase to make his decision. "Leave young Marlowe to me. Stay here and I will have your cloak brought to you. We can then slip away without being seen."

The sense of what he said did not immediately penetrate her disordered thoughts, but as he reached the door she came impulsively to her feet, holding to the chair-back for support.

"But no! Such concern is unnecessary! I have my coachman . . . I cannot allow you . . ."

"Cannot allow?" There was gentle mockery in his voice. He came back to her side, took her firmly by the shoulders, and deposited her once more in the chair. "Now," he said. "Sit there like a good girl and don't argue!"

She felt much too drained to persist.

Gervase meanwhile sought out his hostess and tactfully maneuvered her into a corner where he acquainted her with a brief account of what had happened. "There is no cause for alarm," he replied confidently to her exclamation of distress. "I believe Signorina Merrilli to be suffering from nothing worse than excess of nerves due to rehearsals, lessons, too many parties . . ." He smiled. "Nothing that a good night's sleep won't put right. However"—there was a certain blandness in his voice—"it would save time and a lot of tedious explanation if I might prevail upon you to convey my apologies to Madame St. Austin." And as though the thought had just occurred to him: "Perhaps Lord Marlowe will be good enough to escort her home."

Mrs. Arbuthnot gave him a frank, comprehending look. "His lordship won't love you for usurping his role, Mr. Maxwell."

"I know it, ma'am, but I believe I shall survive. Besides"—his smile deepened a little—"we must consider the signorina's wishes above all else and she . . . does not wish his lordship to be distressed by her indisposition."

"Quite so," said Mrs. Arbuthnot dryly.

Gervase took the hand she extended to him. "I hope I may come again?"

She looked at him for a long moment before giving her abrupt little nod. "You'll be welcome any time. You know that."

Chapter 4

Marissa woke to the rattle of curtain rings along the brass pole as the heavy silk straw-colored curtains were pulled back. Sunlight prodded her eyes and she grunted gently and turned her face into the pillow.

"What time is it?"

"It wants only five minutes to noon and the sun is shining fit to burst itself," Tia Giannina informed her in ringing tones. "Though why the Good God should put himself to so much trouble when half of his creatures are too hard-driven to see and the rest have their aching heads buried in their pillows for most of the daylight hours in order to assuage the rigors of the previous night!" She swept across to the bed and stood with folded arms. "I could have foretold the migraine, had I been consulted, so much coming and going there has been!"

Marissa squinted up at her, rolled over, yawned, and stretched with the unhurried grace of a cat. "You're a dreadful scold, Tia Giannina, do you know that?"

The signorina was undismayed by this observation; having assured herself that all was now well with her charge, she permitted herself only a slight flaring of her magnificent nostrils for answer. "Do you wish breakfast or luncheon?"

Marissa said meekly, "May I have just a little bread and butter . . . and some coffee, perhaps?"

When she had left the room, Marissa lay back with

47

her arms behind her head and her eyes shut. She had slept very much better than was usual after one of her headaches and now felt surprisingly fresh. She frowned slightly. Perhaps some of Mr. Maxwell's strange hypnotic influence was still upon her! Or maybe it had all been a dream.

Certainly, there had been an air of unreality about the whole evening, not least their leavetaking the unobtrusive nature of which had been witnessed by Sir Hugo who, whether by accident or design she knew not, just happened to be lingering at the head of the stairs. He had swept her an elegant leg, expressed dry-voiced commiserations with regard to her indisposition and, with a droll glance at Mr. Maxwell, hoped to find her fully recovered upon the morrow.

Marissa had murmured something incomprehensible, but she rather thought the encounter had annoyed Mr. Maxwell, for he had said little on the journey home and she, very much aware of him close beside her in the swaying vehicle, felt singularly ill-equipped to break the silence. His behavior had been, to say the least, quixotic! If only one might determine its true purpose. That he was a man well used to having his way with women she had recognized in those first moments of meeting; that he was intent upon removing Perry from her unwelcome influence was also apparent—or would it be truer to say that he was intent upon lifting her from under poor trusting Perry's nose and using her for his own ends?

The devil of it was, she could see how easily his object might be achieved if one were not forearmed. His charm was undeniable, even she must recognize that; in the space of one day he had managed to single her out with almost insulting ease; had made her feel (Mother of God defend her) like a wanton, though with luck he had not known how her legs had turned to a jelly! She sternly rebuked her pulse that beat faster at the memory, and a stubbornness grew in her that he should not be permitted to succeed. Perry was too good, too kind to be so casually shrugged aside, and he should not be so used if she had her way.

So intense was her resolve that she quite over-looked the fact that she had already made up her mind not to marry Perry; she was conscious only of that strange lurching sensation which usually came just before she walked out on stage and which was compounded of half fear, half excitement.

The thin, pert maidservant, coming in to spread a white linen cloth over the Boulle table placed in the bow of the window, stared in open admiration at the glowing face of her mistress until Marissa, becoming aware of her interest, came to with a start and threw back the covers, holding out a hand imperiously for her wrapper. The child, overawed, rushed to oblige, ducked a curtsy, and fled.

Marissa, schooling her emotions into compliance, drifted to the window, tying the wrap as she went, and when the door opened again almost immediately to admit Signora Tortinallo, shooing before her a foot-man bearing a tray, she was seemingly absorbed in looking down into the street. She turned as the foot-man left the room and the first thing she saw against the whiteness of the cloth was a single budding rose in a slim fluted silver vase, the outer petals curling away to reveal the deep pulsating crimson of its heart.

Its beauty caught at her throat. "Oh, *cara mia*, what a lovely thought! But I don't remember that vase."

The signora grunted. "And why? Because it arrived this very morning at the door, and without so much as a word to explain it! Flowers we are accustomed to—the hallway is filled with them at this very moment. But all with the card, a letter, even. This"—she stabbed an accusing finger at the rose—"I find ominous in the extreme! Do you have any idea who would express his intentions in such a fashion?"

Oh, yes, Marissa thought. "No, really . . ." she began, while the delicate color stole into her cheeks.

The signora observed it and pursued her interrogation with the zeal of an inquisitor. "The so-handsome gentleman who delivered you with such courtesy into my hands last night, perhaps? So very strange to go out with one gentleman and return with another . . ."

"Mr. Maxwell? Oh, no, it could not be him!" came the too-swift reply, but the signora was busy pursuing her line of thought and failed to notice it.

". . . But then, I tell myself that perhaps you have quarreled with your Lord Marlowe and he is wishful to make amends . . ."

"Truly, Tia Giannina, I don't know!" cried Marissa, half laughing, burying her nose in the rose's fragrance to hide her betraying blushes. "It could be any one of . . . oh, a dozen gentlemen!"

"This is naturally reassuring," said the signora severely. "It is to be hoped that, with so many suitors, you will not be tempted into foolishness."

The story reached Cosmo Pucci, but he wisely refrained from comment when he paid her a visit just as she was finishing her breakfast. She laid aside the concerned little note from Mrs. Arbuthnot that she had been reading and wrinkled her nose at him.

"I am ashamed that you are up and about before me!"

He looked down his strong Italian nose at her. "I should have been displeased to find it otherwise."

"Tia Giannina has been tale-bearing," she said accusingly.

"It was unnecessary," he replied. "You must not underrate my powers of observation, *cara mia*. Because I did not choose to comment when you came to say good night, it does not follow that I was unaware of your state. It was written in your eyes. But to say 'I told you so' at such a moment would have been less than kind, don't you think?"

Their glances locked and hers was the first to fall. "Well, I am fully recovered this morning," she said lightly. "In fact"—indicating the small pile of correspondence beside her plate—"so many people have inquired kindly after me that I feel a complete fraud."

When he made no answer she looked up from sipping her coffee to find his attention fixed pensively upon the rose. "An unknown admirer," she said on a breathless laugh.

"And an eloquent one, withall," he agreed dryly.

He strolled to the window, a slim dapper figure, but she noticed that he leaned more heavily than usual on the gold, crutch-headed cane. After a moment he came and lifted her chin with one of his slim white fingers. Their eyes met.

"You will rest today." It was quietly said, but was a command nonetheless.

"I promise, if you will do likewise," she agreed. And then, urgently. "You will be well enough to attend the first night?"

He frowned briefly and then tapped her cheek in reassurance. "Try to keep me away," he said.

Mr. Maxwell was in his dressing room when it was announced to him that Lord Marlowe was below and most insistent upon seeing him. A faint lift of the eyebrow greeted this intelligence, but he said merely, "Then you had better show his lordship up without delay."

Perry strode into the room without ceremony, his fair good looks, so reminiscent of his sister, marred by a scowl. The sight of Gervase in a superbly frogged dressing gown seated before the mirror of a hand-

51

some rosewood table while his man, Dobson, lovingly burnished the distinguishing silver streaks of his hair did nothing to soothe his exacerbated feelings. He burst into speech.

"Gervase, I have come to ask you to—no, dammit!—to demand an explanation of your behavior. It is not unreasonable in me, I believe, to—to . . ."

"Good morning, Perry," said Gervase blandly, his hand hovering for a moment over the selections of cravats held out to him by his valet. "Do oblige me by sitting down. I will be with you directly." His choice made, he nodded. "Thank you, Dobson."

His movements were sure, unhurried. Perry, with his first flush of rhetoric effectively curtailed, flung himself into a chair. Incensed as he was, however, he could not but admire the deftness of the other's fingers as he made the final crucial adjustments to his handiwork. How often had he tried, sometimes for fully an hour and with any number of crumpled discarded cravats to show, without ever achieving quite that effect.

"And now, Dobson, my coat if you please." Mr. Maxwell stood up. "We decided upon the blue superfine with the mother-of-pearl buttons, I believe . . ."

The dressing gown was discarded, the coat carefully smoothed across the fine shoulders. The valet was dismissed and Gervase turned to regard his young visitor with quiet irony. "Forgive me for keeping you, dear boy, but I am sure you will agree that it is quite impossible to achieve a pleasing result if one's passions are kindled." His glance hovered briefly over Perry's rather mangled neckcloth and his mouth quirked. "You *did* come here to brangle with me, did you not?"

Perry flushed. "Yes. Well, you must see that you made me look so . . . deuced stupid, the way you went off with Marissa last night . . ."

Gervase selected a slim-bladed knife from the table and began to pare his nails. "I am sorry. It was unintentional. Signorina Merrilli felt unwell and wished to leave with the minimum of fuss. I was on hand and offered my services. But surely Mrs. Arbuthnot told you as much?"

"Yes, but . . ." Perry hesitated, made up his mind, and said defiantly, "I'm going to marry her, you know. Marissa, I mean."

Mr. Maxwell lifted his eyes briefly to look at him before returning to survey his hand critically. He put down the knife. "My felicitations, dear boy. When may we expect to see the announcement in the *Gazette*?"

Watching that calm profile, Perry began to feel unaccountably foolish. "Well, as to that, it ain't exactly . . . the thing is, you see, Marissa doesn't want to set the date quite yet."

"Playing hard to get, is she? Now, that is interesting."

"Nothing of the kind!" Perry was indignant. "It is simply that she has engagements to fulfill—and this Signor Pucci, who is her singing teacher, though he appears to wield a great deal too much influence over her, if you ask me . . . she fears he will make difficulties, and so . . . Well, you know how it is . . ."

"I do indeed, dear boy," said Mr. Maxwell softly. So, the singing teacher was in a position of some power? That would bear thinking about. "Still," he said briskly, "you mustn't despair, Perry. I tell you what I'll do. I'll invite Kitty to the first night and you shall make your Marissa known to her."

"I say! Would you? She'd listen to you." Perry was all enthusiasm once more, his grudge forgotten. "And I daresay that when this teacher fellow sees how jolly respectable the whole thing is, he'll change his mind. Wouldn't you say so?"

"Who knows," said Mr. Maxwell equivocally. "One can but try!"

Le Nozze di Figaro opened to find the Opera House's auditorium packed from pit to gallery. Brilliant chandeliers kindled a rich warmth from the red and gold decoration of the boxes as they shimmered with the endless movement of their bejeweled occupants. It was a night of triumph for Marissa, going beyond all her expectations. In her progress through Europe she had made the part of Cherubino very much her own, but tonight she excelled herself as the mischievous Cupid figure at the bottom of every intrigue, forever on the point of ravishment. The audience took her to their hearts, laughing uproariously at the page's follies and sighing in sympathy when the "amorous butterfly's" wings were clipped. Her voice rang pure and clear, showing to advantage against the slightly shrill cadenzas of Madame Brunel's Susanna, and she was obliged to render an encore of the charming aria, "Voi che sapete."

"Well?" Gervase murmured to Kitty under cover of the raptuous final applause. "What do you think of Signorina Merrilli?"

Kitty, dabbing at her eyes with a ridiculous little scrap of cambric, drew a deep breath. "Oh, my dear! I don't know what to say, except that she is indeed lovely and is undoubtedly destined to have all London at her feet! Perhaps"—she lowered her voice still further—"perhaps she will soon be so much in demand that Perry's charms will pall?"

His smile mocked her. Turning to the Misses Phipps he inquired amiably whether they had enjoyed the performance. Miss Hester allowed the whole opera to have been excellently well portrayed; Miss Emily, less inhibited, gave full vent to her pleasure, like a child come to her first party. "Beautiful . . . Truly, truly beautiful!" she exclaimed tremulously. "And Signorina Merrilli . . . what a delightful creature!"

"Would you like to meet her?" he asked. Kitty frowned at him discouragingly, but he feined innocence. "Stay here and I will try to bring her to you before the start of the ballet."

There was direct access to back of the stage from the boxes, subscription to which gave those gentlemen desirous of making assignations with the little charmer of their choice (usually to be found among the opera dancers) a distinct advantage over their less fortunate rivals from the pits. Tonight there was already a considerable crowd jostling enthusiastically for place around the dressing rooms. Marissa's voice rose on that now familiar breathless laugh begging to be given room, and Gervase caught a glimpse of Perry, whose gangling inches set him above the rest, and of Madame Brunel looking decidedly sour as she swept majestically into her own room practically unnoticed.

He made his way through the crowd without difficulty and reached Marissa's dressing room just as the door was about to be closed. He slipped inside on Perry's heels, shutting out the rising chorus of protest, and turned to find Marissa locked with a slim, whitehaired gentleman in a moment of intimacy which effectively excluded everyone else. There was an elegance about this man that claimed one's attention as he stood motionless with Marissa's hands clasped tightly against his cheek. Then with a few murmured words of Italian he kissed the hands and released her.

The giantess of a woman whom Gervase had met briefly when delivering Marissa home on the evening of Mrs. Arbuthnot's party now bustled forward; she produced a chair and Marissa urged the gentleman toward it with a solicitude that was touching. Only when he was settled did she appear to notice that anyone was there other than Perry.

She came across the room, her shamelessly painted jade eyes still brilliant with the exhilaration of her success. The page's costume became her slender figure to such pefection that Gervase would have been less than human had he not used the moment to advantage.

"Mr. Maxwell!" He withdrew his gaze reluctantly from contemplation of her shapely leg and even more shapely ankle to find her exhilaration simmering into indignation. In an embarrassed, almost pleading way she mouthed, "Please!" and then aloud, "How . . . unexpected."

He was decorum itself as he bowed over her hand and complimented her upon her performance, but his eyes laughed wickedly at her in the moment before he veiled them.

"You must allow me to introduce you to my dear cousin and teacher, Signor Pucci. Cosmo, this is Mr. Maxwell, who is . . . a friend of Perry." Her hesitation was hardly perceptible, yet both men were aware of it as they exchanged punctilious greetings.

Tia Giannina, who had vanished from sight behind a lacquered screen, now emerged bearing a wrap embroidered with splendid jade-green dragons into which she hustled her charge with such unseemly haste that Marissa dared not look at Mr. Maxwell as she said weakly, "And Signora Tortinallo you have already met, I think."

Gervase was treated to a fulminating stare and a rumble of recognition from somewhere inside the vast bosom. This he acknowledged with impeccable courtesy and returned his attention to Signor Pucci whom he found assessing him with the same thoroughness that he himself usually accorded to possible rivals—a disconcerting experience, and one that he overcame by saying equably, "Your pupil does you great credit, signor. She has more than fulfilled that promise evinced at her initial debut."

A gleam of interest showed in the older man's eyes. "You were there, in Milan, Mr. Maxwell?"

"I was, indeed, signor, and am now delighted to have had my opinions of that night confirmed."

He knew that Marissa was staring at him accusingly. "You never once mentioned that you had seen me before!"

"Did I not?" he said innocently. "How very remiss of me!"

Perry looked from one to the other and began to feel excluded. He said in hushed tones, his face aflush with eagerness, "I thought you were magnificent tonight! And I dare swear there ain't a soul present who'd say otherwise." He looked as though he would like to have said much more, but instead he moved impulsively across to the great bower of flowers in one corner of the room and lifted the card from an enormous vase of pink roses. "They arrived safely, I see," he said shyly.

"Thank you, yes. They are very beautiful."

Involuntarily, Marissa's glance was drawn to the place where, overshadowed by the rest, a solitary crimson rose reposed in a silver holder. Perry followed the direction of her glance.

"Lord, that's a bit paltry!" he exclaimed with another smug look at his own offering. He peered closer. "It ain't too hard to figure why the sender don't care to put his name to it."

Marissa looked Gervase squarely in the eye. "What do you think, Mr. Maxwell?"

"Me?" He purported to be taken aback by the question. "Oh, I suspect that your unknown admirer is shy," he ventured, straight-faced. "Truth to tell, I find the simplicity of his offering rather endearing."

She almost choked. "And romantic, would you say?"

"Oh, definitely romantic. Incorrigibly so," he agreed, watching with interest as a pink flush suffused her cheek. "But speaking of admirers, I wonder would you grant a favor?" She eyed him warily. "I have with me Perry's sister, also two rather elderly spinster ladies who are neighbors of hers in Hill Street . . ."

"What? Not the Misses Phipps," Perry exclaimed. "Lord, Gervase, whatever possessed you to saddle yourself with those two quaint old antidotes?"

"My dear boy, you must not be so unkind about Miss Hester and Miss Emily . . ."

"I don't mean to be." Perry grinned. "Matter of fact, I'm particularly fond of old Emily! She used to feed me sweetmeats on the sly when I was a boy—gave me money too, sometimes . . ."

"Be quiet, Perry," Mr. Maxwell admonished sternly. "The thing is, it would give these ladies—all of them—particular pleasure to meet you, signorina, but I really feel that I could not subject the two Misses Phipps to the hazards of a backstage visit . . ."

"No, of course not."

"And I wondered if you would consent, with Perry and myself for escort, to attend them in my box. It is quite close to the stage."

Just what game *was* this provoking man playing, Marissa wondered. He had made no attempt to see her since the night of Mrs. Arbuthnot's party, though she was as sure as she could be that he was the sender of the roses, which had come each day since. And now, just when she had girded herself up to do battle with him, here he was, apparently aiding and abetting Perry in his cause! It ought to be reassuring; instead she was filled with disquiet.

"Do say you will come, Marissa!" Perry's pleading broke into her thoughts. "I'd most awfully like you and Kitty to meet!"

She turned helplessly to Cosmo. He could not pretend enthusiasm, but now was not the time to risk antagonizing persons of influence. "If the crowd has dispersed and Mr. Maxwell will vouch that you come to no harm, then I permit," he said.

In the event, everything went well; only a few hopefuls still lingered near the door and they were easily dealt with. Kitty, as Gervase had always supposed she would be when the moment came, was her own charming gracious self; she was unwittingly aided by Miss Emily who was so overcome and twittered with such birdlike persistence that only the most fragmented of conversations was possible.

They were on the point of leaving when Marissa said impulsively, "We are holding a small celebration supper party in Arlington Street later this evening, Lady Kilroy—just for a few friends, you understand. It would please me greatly if you could feel yourself able to come."

Kitty was taken aback, hesitated, and cast a swift look at Gervase who returned it enigmatically. Marissa noted the interchange, and wondered at it. Kitty was thus obliged to make her own decision.

"Thank you," she said a trifle awkwardly. "It is most kind of you, but I believe I must refuse. Miss Hester and Miss Emily have already invited me to take a dish of tea with them when we return home and I would not care to disappoint them." She smiled in mitigation. "Another time, perhaps."

"Yes, of course." All color had gone out of Marissa's voice.

"Am I invited to supper, signorina?" Gervase murmured provocatively as they waited for Perry who had been detained by Miss Emily.

"Certainly, if you wish it." Marissa was less than encouraging. "But do you not also have to take tea?"

"Perhaps, but that will hardly occupy the whole

evening. The old ladies will be for their beds e'er long!"

"And Lady Kilroy?" The tone had now grown distinctly frigid. "Does she also retire early? Strange, but I would not have thought it!"

"Don't make hasty judgments, my dear young lady." He wagged an admonishing finger under her nose. "Lady Kilroy's reservations are perfectly understandable. Her brother's happiness means a great deal to her and, though you may not be aware of it, Perry was on the verge of becoming betrothed to the daughter of an old family friend when he met you."

"I do know, as it happens," she said defiantly. "But there was no definite agreement . . ."

"Is that what he told you? Well, why not, indeed? By now, I daresay he has convinced himself that it is so." He leaned one shoulder against the wall, arms folded, his eyes glinting down at her in the soft light of the passage. "And whatever the truth, one cannot bring oneself to quarrel with his taste."

The drawled observation made her flinch. "You make me sound . . ."

"Yes?" he said softly. "How do I make you sound?"

Marissa shook her head, not wanting to put it into words.

"Do you intend to marry Lord Marlowe?"

The directness of his question brought her chin up. "Do you intend to prevent me?" she retorted.

There was not light enough to be sure, but she rather thought his eyes narrowed slightly. There was no alteration in his voice, however.

"Now, why should I wish to do that?"

"To please Lady Kilroy," she suggested hardly.

She had provoked a definite reaction at last, but it was not quite the one she expected. He straightened up and took her chin lightly between thumb and forefinger so that she was obliged to look into his eyes.

"Oh, no!" he said. "*If* I decide to take you from Perry, it will be to please myself."

His sheer audacity almost robbed her of breath, but not quite. "And what of me?" she demanded. "This . . . arrogant speculation must surely presuppose that I would allow myself to be *taken from Perry*, as you so charmingly put it?" She smiled sweetly up at him. "Or may I expect to be abducted?"

"Certainly not," he said on the ghost of a laugh. "I have never yet been obliged to ravish anyone and it would be a little ridiculous to begin at my age, don't you think?"

"I think this whole conversation is ridiculous, and better forgotten," she said, grasping at sanity. "I will not play your game, Mr. Maxwell, so you may stop sending me your roses, and . . .

"My what?"

His air of puzzlement did not deceive her for one moment. She was about to rush into speech again when Perry, having managed at last to extricate himself from Miss Emily's verbal entanglements, began a strategic retreat from the box.

Marissa seized the opportunity, released herself from his grasp, and turned to await Perry.

"You know very well!" she whispered furiously over a defensively hunched shoulder.

The echo of a laugh was his only reply.

Chapter 5

The weeks that followed confirmed Marissa as a singer of exceptional qualities. The *Times* wrote glowingly: "In Signorina Merrilli the opera has found a treasure indeed. Not only is her every gesture a delight to behold, her voice as lyrically pleasing to the ear as it is perfectly pitched; Merrilli also possesses that indefinable quality which enables her to move an audience to laughter and in the next moment to tears. May she grace our theaters for many years to come."

She was presented to the Regent who came twice to see her, and was so enchanted that he insisted she must come to sing for him at Carlton House, for which honor she was indebted to Mr. Maxwell, who had persuaded Prinny to attend the opera and indeed had accompanied him on both occasions. Marissa, faced with the prospect of being obliged to express her gratitude to him (with his sardonic eye upon her) found herself stumbling over the words.

"It was nothing," he said with mock modesty. "It needed but a word and I, perforce, was the one privileged to utter it."

It seemed to Marissa that Mr. Maxwell had taken to visiting the house in Arlington Street with a disturbing frequency. It made little difference that he was only one of many who came now that her success was assured; nor did it reassure her that he came mostly with Celestine and Rupert, and devoted most of his time to conversing amiably with Cosmo Pucci, who was delighted to find him so knowledgeable about Italy, for she occasionally surprised a look in his eyes when they met hers across the room which unsettled her, recalling, as it was clearly intended to do, their recent conversation at the theater. And, if *that* were not enough, there was the unresolved matter of the roses which still arrived daily, providing Tia Giannina with endless scope for conjecture.

There were many admirers from whom she might choose, for the house was in a fair way to becoming a popular venue and most days Signor Pucci found the peace of his drawing room invaded. He bore the intrusion with equanimity, rejoicing to see how much Marissa was now in demand.

"It is really quite extraordinary," he told Gervase. "Some days I scarcely see anything of her. It is to be hoped that she does not overtax her energies."

Gervase looked across the room to where Marissa moved restlessly between one group and another conversing in animated fashion, now laughing teasingly up at Perry, who was never far away, now leaning down to confide some morsel of gossip to Celestine.

"The signorina looks to be in splendid spirits!" he observed dryly.

"Oh, Marissa responds to her success, as she does to all things which capture her interest, with total enthusiasm! But it is this very wholeheartedness which makes her so vulnerable. I try to guard her affairs with vigilance, Mr. Maxwell, for she is ripe to be exploited—and thereafter, hurt." Signor Pucci shook his head. "But I tell you, it is no easy task and sometimes I doubt that I am any longer able to serve Marissa as I would wish. Every day we receive requests that she will do this concert or perform at some function. Mr. Elliston of Drury Lane came personally to beg Marissa to consider taking the role of the Don in his revival of a short masterpiece, an amusing travesty entitled *Don Giovanni in London* . . ."

It was clear from Signor Pucci's expression that he was not much taken with the idea. Gervase wondered if he was aware that there were already ballad sheets being sold on the streets, proclaiming with bawdy eloquence the undoubted shapeliness of Merrilli's legs; he would certainly have been less than pleased if he had heard the outspoken comments of that old reprobate, General FitzAlbert at White's on the previous evening, on a similar theme.

"You do not approve?" he asked blandly and saw a faint look of distaste pass across the fastidious features.

"Mr. Elliston assured me that it is an innocuous piece designed to please the public, but I cannot accept that such an appearance will in any laudable way advance Marissa's reputation in the theater; already, every artist of note vies for the privilege of taking her likeness"—the lips twisted a trifle cynically—"which they will no doubt distribute later at a handsome profit among her many admirers!"

It seemed to Gervase that the signor minded rather more than a mere cousin ought, or a teacher for his pupil, even. As his visits continued, he found himself studying the relationship with an almost obsessive interest, and the more he did so, the more he became aware that a very special bond existed between the two; but whether it extended beyond the bounds of mere affection he could not determine and was annoyed with himself that the answer should matter so much.

Marissa meanwhile was enjoying her success to the full, unaware of the concern being generated about her. Had she known of Cosmo's fears, she might have reassured him, for experience had taught her to be wary of too much adulation. But it was very agreeable nonetheless to be so sought-after, to be showered with presents, some which made her gasp a little by virtue of their sheer extravagance, and some which she was obliged to decline kindly, but firmly, where it appeared likely that the benefactor might require of her something more than an eloquent expression of thanks.

It was particularly flattering to be feted by those ladies of the *haut ton* who would normally accord her nothing more than a frosty smile, but for whom, suddenly, the success of a musical soiree could not be guaranteed if Merrilli did not honor it however briefly with her presence. However, Marissa was in no danger of being deceived into mistaking tolerance for genuine acceptance; for the present she was in demand—the *dernier cri*—a plaything of the fashionable, but she knew from experience that tomorrow or the next day some new fad would take their fancy and she would be discarded with as little thought as yesterday's crumpled gown. She said as much to Celestine as they returned home after one such afternoon engagement.

"So? Should that trouble you?" Celestine shrugged her elegant little shoulders and continued blithely as Marissa shook her head. "Me, they would dearly love to shun, for I am not at all respectable." She grinned. "But I am fortunate in that I have in my past a great uncle who was a French Duke of the Blood Royal, though he is long dead—and so they are obliged to accept me!"

"I fear I cannot lay claim to any such illustrious ancestor."

Something in her voice made Celestine glance at her curiously. "Forgive me, *chérie*—you never speak of your past and perhaps it is that you do not wish to do so, but I have often wondered . . ."

"I don't mind speaking about it," Marissa said

slowly. "I suppose my thoughts seldom go back nowadays beyond my life with Cosmo. I have been with him since I was fifteen, when my mother died . . ."

"She was Italian?"

Marissa nodded, twisting the strings of her reticule. "And very beautiful. Not strong, physically, you know, but oh, *Dio*, she could be stubborn!" Laughter bubbled up at the memory. "Do you know, she refused to learn any but the most basic English phrases? I practically grew up speaking Italian, for we lived in a fairly isolated house in the country, near Dublin. The only English I knew had a strong Irish flavor, picked up from the servants."

"And your father?"

Marissa's head lifted. "Ah, my father! Well, I hardly knew him, but according to Cosmo, he was a feckless charmer who swept Mama off her feet, and having taken her to Ireland, neglected her most shamefully and came to a bad end years later, kicked in the head by one of his own horses."

"But how dreadful!"

"Perhaps Cosmo was biased, for I am sure he was in love with Mama himself and never forgave the man who took her from him." Marissa's eyes grew soft. "But I think Mama never forgot him, either, for when she was near death she wrote to him and he came and carried me back to his home in Venice." She swung around to face Celestine with shining eyes. "Anything I am now I owe to Cosmo—he was father and mother and dear friend to me and I can never repay him for all the happiness he has brought to my life these past few years. I just wish you could have known him before his illness. He was like quicksilver! It is still there in his eyes sometimes, but . . ."

Celestine watched the vivid expressive features and wondered, like Gervase and many others, probably, about the nature of the relationship between these

66

cousins. It was not simply a teacher and pupil ar-
rangement, though that came into it; the disparity in
age did not preclude something of a more intimate
nature—it would not be so uncommon an arrange-
ment, after all, but it was something that one could
not question and Marissa never gave one the least
hint...

"Have you ever thought, *chérie*, what you would
do, if . . . ?" The moment Celestine had opened her
mouth she wished the words unsaid; as her voice pe-
tered out, there lay between them an awkward
silence, Celestine biting her lip and seeing the curiously stricken look in her friend's eyes. "I am a fool,"
she chastized herself bitterly, "and besides, it is none
of my business!"

"I do not mind that you ask." Marissa's voice
trembled and firmed again. "It would be stupid to
pretend that I have not wondered how I should go on
without Cosmo. I suppose I should continue to sing—
it is the only thing I know."

"Or get married, perhaps?"

"Or get married," she agreed equivocally.

It was clear that Celestine still felt badly about her
want of tact and Marissa was searching desperately in
her mind for some way to give her thoughts a new
direction when she saw two familiar figures on horse-
back cantering toward them.

"Mr. Maxwell!" Marissa looked him challengingly
in the eyes and received a droll smile by return. "And
Major Egerton! You are come in the nick of time," she
said gaily. "We have been discussing the future and
are in danger of growing excessively morbid."

"Fustian! My dear signorina," Rupert said. "What
could you possibly find to depress your spirits? There
can be few people with so brilliant a future ahead of
them! Eh, Gervase?"

Marissa was very conscious of Mr. Maxwell as he

murmured assent. His searching glance, she was sure, would miss little of her mood. She became defiantly gay, the words tumbled over themselves in her anxiety to prove to him how little he need trouble himself.

Then she turned to Major Egerton. "Ah, that is very well for the present but only consider how it will be many years from now. I shall probably grow fat like Madame Brunel"—she pulled a ferocious face which made Celestine laugh—"and scowl at each new young singer who comes to threaten my position!"

"Is she *so* resentful?"

"Oh, no! But you must understand that she and Tia Giannina are the bitterest enemies. It is much more amusing than anything happening on the stage, I promise you! Just lately I have mislaid one or two small things—nothing of importance, you understand—a glove, perhaps, or the smallest of brooches, but for all the fuss it has caused you would think it a tragedy of the first order—and has given rise to some of the greatest dramatic scenes ever enacted!"

She launched into a full demonstration on the spot and a lone rider passing by looked nervously in her direction, as though he had by mistake entered Bedlam. She paused to smile reassuringly at him and he took off at a gallop. She shrugged, cleared her throat and began.

"Firstly we have Tia Giannina, muttering a long and involved recitative into the folds of her chin, much concerned with the untrustworthy nature of the servants some prima donnas are wont to employ! At which point Madame Brunel thrusts out her ample bosom, *so* . . ." She attempted to adopt the good Madame's stance with hands clasped to her breast and arms akimbo, to such effect that Rupert was almost helpless with laughter.

"A-hah!" she replied, in an aria rich with cadenzas. "A dresser of such proportions that she can hardly squeeze through the door, let alone turn around in so small a room, could be guaranteed to sweep almost anything to the floor and thence carry it to perdition beneath her skirts!"

Celestine wiped her eyes. "Oh, *chérie!* That was quite wickedly accurate!"

"Madame Brunel to the life," Rupert agreed weakly.

Marissa looked to Mr. Maxwell.

He had watched her all the while, a dry fleeting smile about his lips. In her dress of sprigged muslin, crisp and simple, and with the deep poke of her bonnet lined with palest pink ruched silk framing the mischievous face so becomingly, she looked like a child dressed up to perform for her elders. And yet he could have sworn that those beguiling eyes had held tears in those first few moments of meeting. There was no trace of them now, however; her party piece at an end, she was once more the sophisticated young opera singer ready to parry any comment he might offer. It would be a pity to disappoint her.

"Highly entertaining," he said. "But the picture you paint of your future alarms me. I hope you don't mean to dedicate your life exclusively to the theater? More than one gentleman's passion will be doomed to wither away unrequited if you do! And that would be a tragedy, don't you agree?"

"I am sure I should be very sorry for any gentleman thus afflicted," she said lightly. "But you surely cannot expect me to requite them all?"

Rupert chuckled. "She has a point there, Gervase."

"So how am I to choose?" Marissa persisted. "Perhaps Mr. Maxwell would care to advise me?"

The look of innocent inquiry which accompanied this last brought a quirk of humor to his face, but undaunted he said that he would not presume, for he was sure there was very little that he could teach the signorina in such matters. In this spirit of gentle banter the journey home passed very agreeably.

Marissa had scarcely been admitted at the door when Signora Tortinallo appeared on the stair, intoning in a whisper that could be heard all the way down to the servants' hall below. "There has been a gentleman closeted with the Maestro in the drawing room for this hour past. You are to go in the moment you arrive!"

"Who is it—do you know?" Marissa whispered back, lifting her skirts to take the stairs at a run under the signora's disapproving eye.

"But of course! How should I not know? Such a fine impressive gentleman he is. And such manners! It is Sir Hugo Severin." Marissa's frown brought a sharp reaction. "You do not like Sir Hugo?"

"I . . . hardly know him. What can he want with Signor Pucci?"

"It is to do with an opera that is to be specially written for you," said the signora with complacence as they reached the landing.

Marissa feigned shock. "Tia Giannina! You have been listening at the door!"

"Can I be blamed if the gentleman broadcasts his business to the air? Come now, and let me take your bonnet and shawl, you can then make yourself tidy . . ." But she spoke to herself, for Marissa was already at the drawing room door and closing it behind her.

"Ah, my dear, there you are at last." Cosmo Pucci extended a hand. "You are acquainted with Sir Hugo, I believe?"

Severin had risen at her entry and he now made her an elegant leg. He was dressed faultlessly as ever, in blue coat and buff pantaloons. The high starched points of his collar drew attention to his rather florid features, but his eyes dwelt with intense interest upon her becomingly flushed face and his manner was irreproachably suave as he hoped that he found her well.

"Yes, thank you, except that I am exhausted!" Marissa loosed the ribbons of her bonnet and sank gratefully onto a nearby chair. "Mrs. Grantham's musical afternoon was such a squeeze that one could scarcely breathe in that tiny room, let alone sing. I am sure I wonder where all the people come from!"

"Ah, but you have only to consider the reward they reap for some small discomfort, signorina," said Sir Hugo with his thin smile. "They come, after all, for the joy of meeting you and hearing your exquisite voice."

He seated himself again on the sofa opposite Signor Pucci and looked at him with something of expectancy.

"Sir Hugo has come with a most interesting and, I may say, generous proposition, my dear." Signor Pucci's voice was as measured as ever, but his eyes betrayed an unusual animation. "You remember the young composer, Perchon, whose work we so admired in Paris last year?"

"Yes, of course. He wrote that charming little oratorio which we performed for the King's birthday."

"Just so, *cara mia.* Well, it seems that he was equally impressed with you. In fact, he begs that he may be allowed the privilege of writing an opera especially for you."

Marissa rose and went to perch on the chair at his side, one arm clasped about his shoulder. "But how ...?" She looked across at Sir Hugo.

"How am I concerned? It is, you might say, an accident of fate, signorina." His hand described a graceful, self-effacing gesture. "I have for several years now been one of Frederick Perchon's patrons. He came to London recently for the sole purpose of hearing you sing—and to crave my support in the matter of this opera, which I should tell you is already half completed." Sir Hugo played idly with one of the fobs adorning the gold chain which lay across his waistcoat. "It would make him very happy if you would accept it."

"But, of course! I will be delighted to accept!" Marissa cried, hugging Cosmo, and in her excitement, leaning forward, eyes shining, her lips eagerly parted. "And the theme, sir . . . do you know the theme?"

Severin, watching her, was secretly exultant. She was going to be so grateful to him. He would make very sure of that! But with Pucci's eyes on him, he was all decorum. "It is dramatic in content, and is set in ancient Greece—a story of unrequited love, I believe—always popular with an audience! I see no reason why it should not be ready to go on in the autumn."

"Oh, but . . ." Marissa's face clouded; she glanced uncertainly at Cosmo. "We had not intended to stay beyond the summer. Signor Pucci's health . . ."

"My dear child, you fuss too much!" He put up a hand to pat the one gripping his shoulder so tightly. "I am much improved, as you can see. And what is a few weeks? There will be time enough before the winter comes."

It was true, she thought. He *was* better, as she had told Celestine. He was less tired, less inclined to be out of breath. Perhaps it was the onset of warmer weather or simply that her success had given him new strength. If so, maybe this latest opportunity would do him more good than anything.

Perry received her news with mixed feelings. A new opera in the autumn would put off once again any decision about their marriage. Already her increasing popularity and the commitments it brought with it were severely curtailing the amount of time they could be together.

"And besides," he said, "I'm not at all sure I care for the idea of your being beholden to Severin!"

She laughed at his vehemence. "Well, you need have no fear. Sir Hugo is the composer's patron, nothing more. I am grateful to him for giving me this chance, of course, but I am not in the least attracted to him, I assure you."

It was an afternoon in early June, one of the few afternoons when she was free and he had carried her off for a picnic in the Surrey woods. They sat on a carpet of moss in dappled sunlight, nibbling on cold chicken and drinking champagne and talking a lot of agreeable nonsense until the talk had come back inevitably to the subject that most obsessed him.

He lifted his head suddenly to look up at her. "Oh, dearest Marissa! I do so adore you! And I get so afraid that you'll grow tired of me."

There was so much anguish in his voice that she could only look at him helplessly. She ought never to have let things go this far, she reproached herself. He was only two years her junior but there was an emotional gulf so wide between them that she couldn't find the words to bridge it; to tell him that what he felt was mere infatuation, and would pass, was too painful to contemplate. It was her own selfish desire to be put upon a pedestal and worshiped that had made Perry her slave and it was incumbent upon her to find some way to extricate herself without hurting his pride. A pair of dark, sardonic eyes came unbidden into her mind—oh, how he would delight in her predicament if only he knew!

Chapter 6

"I am invited to Mrs. Arbuthnot's villa for the coming weekend." Marissa laid the letter down on the breakfast table and glanced across to where Cosmo sat in a comfortable chair near the open window. The sun was already warm; the cry of a street vendor drifted in now and then upon the gentlest of breezes which came to lift the newspaper he was reading.

He looked up. "Do you wish to go?"

She gave him an affectionate, half-rueful smile. "It would be rather pleasant, I think—if you wouldn't mind!" A graceful, deprecating gesture assured her that he would not. "I don't have any engagements until Tuesday, and it is so quiet and peaceful at Chiswick, near the river. You know, I have been wondering if we should not look for a little house—somewhere not too far from London. It would be sensible for you to get out of the town. Soon it is going to be very warm and not healthy, they tell me."

"That, I am used to," he said. "But I will think about it. A house in the country might be most agreeable for the summer months." He glanced down again. "This newspaper, the *Morning Post*—the theater critic thinks very well of your performance. He is almost fulsome in his praise!"

Marissa rose and went to lean over his chair, one hand resting on his shoulder. He reached up and covered it with his own as she read.

"But wait until we can presently astound them with

74

our very own opera, eh? With melodies that will exploit the true range of your voice to the full!"

Monsieur Perchon had already called upon them. He had seemed an insignificant little man beside the elegant Sir Hugo, slighter even than she had remembered. But as soon as he began to speak about his music, all diffidence vanished and his thin, pale face radiated enthusiasm. The score, as far as he had taken it, was more than promising and it had been arranged that he would come to Arlington Street whenever he wished, so that Signor Pucci might follow the work's progress closely and perhaps offer advice.

"So," Signor Pucci said, putting down the newspaper and leaning aside a little so that he might look at Marissa. "It is settled. You will go to Chiswick." And dryly, "Does Lord Marlowe go also?"

"I think not. He has been summoned to visit his mother who is unwell, and as the family home is a considerable distance away, it is unlikely that he will return for several days."

Marissa did not add that this was a source of some relief to her. A quiet weekend with a few friends, Mrs. Arbuthnot had said in her letter ("You won't be called upon to sing a single note if you don't wish it!"). The prospect was immensely appealing, and indeed the day of the journey, dawning crystal clear, with only a puffy white cloud here and there to lend emphasis to the blue of the sky, seemed to auger well for the whole enterprise.

She felt rather like a small child being packed off to stay with strangers, so much fuss did Signora Tortinallo make over what was to be taken.

"The *mousseline de soie* you must have, for it is of a lightness should the weather grow hot, and the blossom crepe becomes you greatly. Also, there is your amber half-dress—and the new spotted muslin together with the embroidered chambric for the mornings. And, of course, you will need your riding habit, for doubtless this Mrs. Arbuthnot will keep horses for the riding . . ."

"Tia Giannina, stop, I beg of you, or I shall grow quite dizzy! I am only to be away two days—three at the most. And it will be a very informal gathering!"

"So?" the signora demanded to be told. "This then requires that you do not dress?"

"No—yes, well, of course, one must dress, but as and how one pleases!"

"Then it pleases me that you look well! Though how you are to manage without me, I cannot think!" A sigh of enormous proportion shook the signora's frame. "That child Maria who goes with you knows nothing of your ways!"

"Oh, come, I am not *so* difficult, I hope!" Marissa hid a smile, knowing well that Tia Giannina dearly wished to be going in Maria's place; only her loyalty to her beloved maestro kept her from it.

As Celestine was also going to Chiswick, it seemed sensible that they should travel together. Rupert, another of Mrs. Arbuthnot's guests, was to make his own way later. "There is some horrid prize fight he must attend," she explained with a grimace.

"Do you know how many we are to be?" Marissa asked her when Arlington Street was left behind.

"My dear, I have no idea, but no more than eight to ten people. Certainly Mathilda does not care for more on these occasions."

"You will have been invited quite often I suppose? And Rupert, also?"

The question was casually put; Celestine's reply, that they had been several times and had found it a most enjoyable experience, proved less than satisfactory. What Marissa really wanted to know was whether she might expect to find Mr. Maxwell one of the number, but she did not wish to appear partial. Their paths had begun to cross with disturbing frequency of late, and though his attentions were never obtrusive, he managed to make her very much aware of his presence. She even had the horridest notion that he enjoyed doing so and was simply biding his time until he was ready to take his campaign a stage further. But this was fanciful thinking and she thrust it from her.

Mrs. Arbuthnot greeted them warmly and led them through at once to a large saloon decorated very much in the French style with a white and gold compartmented ceiling, at the center of which four flying cherubs supported a massive gilt chandelier. Gilt was very much in evidence also in the furniture with several ornate Louis Quinze commodes and a scattering of sofas and chairs, gilt-backed and upholstered in pale blue silk. Long windows were thrown open to a balustraded terrace beyond which stretched lush green lawns, leading to a rose garden that was a riot of bloom. In the near distance could be seen a small cupola set gracefully among trees, and a curving stonework bridge passed over a stream diverted from the river to flow chuckling over pebbles across the garden and back to the river once more.

Several chairs were set out on the terrace beneath an awning and here reclined Lady Drusilla Oakwood, an amiably vague widow of some five-and-thirty summers, who shared Mrs. Arbuthnot's enthusiasm for good works. Mr. James Gardiner and his young sister, Clare, were also known slightly to Marissa, and the very tall, very thin exquisite man strolling across the lawn was a Lord Ravensdale, the beautiful young woman on his arm, Baroness Leidl, who spoke almost no English.

"But who needs to speak with such looks!" Celestine sighed irreverently.

But there was no Mr. Maxwell. Marissa told herself that it must be the heat of the afternoon which made her feel inexplicably flat.

"Such a pity that Lord Marlowe's mama was taken unwell, my dear," Mrs. Arbuthnot said later as she waved away the various waiting servants and walked with Marissa to her bedchamber, Celestine having chosen to remain a little longer on the terrace. "Still, we mustn't allow that to spoil a fine weekend, eh?" She stopped before a door. "I hope you'll like this room. It seemed to me it would be just right for you."

There were cool green walls and a glowing yellow counterpane; a beautiful Venetian pier glass above a figured walnut dressing table—and on the wall opposite the bed, a painting. She recognized the scene at once—a junction of two canals situated near their home in Venice. In the picture golden sunlight was striking the wall of an old palazzo, lighting up the crumbled carvings on its worn surface and below, like a shadow on the opaque, sheening water, a gondola lay motionless. So faithful was the reproduction that for a moment Marissa's eyes pricked with homesickness.

"Oh, yes!" She sighed softly. "It is quite perfect!"

"Good." Mrs. Arbuthnot nodded, satisfied. "I'll leave you, then. Remember, you must feel free to do exactly as you please. And if there's anything at all you want, you've only to mention it, either to me or to that butler of mine, Watts." Her eyes gleamed. "He doesn't have half enough to do! We dine at six. By then, our little party should be complete."

Marissa rested for a while, enjoying the faint sounds that came through the open windows—composed of birdsong, the occasional rustle of leaves, and the distant murmur of water. She allowed them to settle her into consciousness. Then she rose and dressed. Perhaps influenced by her surroundings, she chose a high-waisted gown in her favorite pale green and very much Venetian in design—of embroidered silk open down the front over a cream slip, the sleeves puffed and slashed to display the rich cream lining. Maria, who had burst into floods of tears upon seeing the picture so evocative of her home, recovered herself sufficiently to assist her mistress and, though less skilled than Tia Giannina, managed to achieve a pleasing knot of hair falling into a tumble of curls, through which she threaded a pretty gold fillet.

There was time and to spare when she was ready. Since Mrs. Arbuthnot had been at great pains to allow of one's being able to do exactly as one pleased, she decided it would be pleasant to spend a little more time out of doors—a stroll on the terrace, perhaps even a brief exploration of the garden. Downstairs she was met by the efficiently hovering Watts to whom she conveyed her intention. He would inform Madam when she came down, he assured her, and went before her to open the saloon door.

The windows still stood open. The sun was past its zenith and shedding a mellow glow across the garden as she wandered out to lean upon the parapet of the terrace. There was a feeling of inevitability as a figure silently unfurled itself from one of the chairs and came to stand beside her, a white cravat gleaming against a dark evening coat. Her heart leapt and steadied.

"Good evening, Mr. Maxwell," she said without a tremor, without even turning to look at him.

"Signorina." The familiar voice was laconic. "You don't seem very surprised to find me here."

"I have ceased to be surprised by anything you do," she said loftily. "A man who continues to send roses when he had been several times entreated to stop will do anything!"

"Dear me! Do they still come?" He evinced surprise. "Perhaps you should reconsider your attitude. So devoted a suitor is surely worthy of some reward—if only for his persistence!"

Marissa had resolved to remain severe, but laughter came bubbling up as she turned to face him. "I do wish you will be serious! I know very well that it is you who sends them—" His eyebrow quirked upward with an air of pained innocence. "It is most embarrassing for me, and besides, Tia Giannina is fast running out of places where she may store those pretty silver holders. One cannot simply throw them out!"

"Whyever not?" he said carelessly. "They have served their purpose."

She gasped. "It is well she cannot hear you! Such extravagance would shock her to the core!"

"There is, of course, a much simpler means of resolving your problem."

It had been a mistake to look at him; his eyes danced with deviltry, and though she knew it would be sheer folly to encourage him in his foolishness, a heady intoxication was already beginning to oust common sense.

She said weakly, "Mr. Maxwell, if you have somehow arranged this weekend in order to pursue *that* line of reasoning . . ."

"Signorina *mia*," he said softly, "you surely cannot suppose for one moment that Mrs. Arbuthnot would connive (such a disagreeable word!) at anything of the kind?"

"Not knowingly, but oh, I have seen sufficient of you, sir, to be convinced that if you want something badly enough, you will find the means to achieve it!" Her face colored most becomingly at the implication of what she had just said. He noted the fact and took the hand which clung to the parapet as though it were a lifeline. He smoothed its trembling with one slim sensuous thumb.

"Mr. Maxwell, I . . . please release my hand," she said in a most odd voice.

"At once, my dear." He dropped a kiss lightly in the palm, closed her fingers over it, and gave it back to her. "There. Shall we go inside? I expect it is the evening air that makes you tremble." He took her arm solicitously, but the devil was still in his eyes. "Or can it be that you do not trust yourself to be two whole days in my company without succumbing to the lure of my irresistible charm?"

Marissa realized how far she had betrayed herself and sought desperately to retrieve her position, half laughed, bit her lip, and said rallyingly, "Oh, as to that, signor, I have no qualms. I have been subjected in the past few years, to almost every predatory trick, every attempt at seduction, every fascination nuance of flattery yet devised by man! I am therefore reasonably confident of being able to withstand two days of even your undoubted charm!"

His eyes did not lose their gleam, but they narrowed, raking her face. "I don't know if you are a gambler, signorina," he said, "but that sounds to me remarkably like a challenge!"

She found that she still had her fingers clasped tightly over the tingling imprint of his kiss and hastily released them. Her mind rejected totally the stupidity of entering into any kind of contest with him, yet something inside her, something infinitely more primitive, was reluctant to put period to what could at the very least be termed a dangerously stimulating game.

She heard Rupert's voice in the saloon, coming nearer. "You must interpret it as you please," she said, and the die was cast.

Quite what she expected she wasn't sure. In the event, that first evening passed so pleasantly that she began to wonder if Mr. Maxwell had thought better of the whole thing. He was at his most charming, but though he singled her out for attention, there was none of the mockery she had come to associate with their exchanges, and she responded with a lively wit that called for very little effort on her part. Several times she saw Celestine look at them curiously, but she said nothing.

"Do you ride as well as you sing, signorina?" he murmured, under cover of leading her to the stairs as good nights were said.

"Certainly, sir," she returned playfully. "My father was, after all, a breeder of horses."

His look was quizzical. "Shall we say eight o'clock, then? While all these sluggards are still abed."

She was downstairs on the stroke of eight, the skirt of her amber riding habit looped over her arm displaying a glimpse of kid half-boots. Mr. Maxwell was already there, awaiting her. His eyes moved appreciatively over her trim, close-fitting jacket worn with a snowy lace cravat, a high-crowned black hat set primly over her eyes.

The horses were ready for them and soon they were cantering along by the river in a companionable silence. The morning air was like wine, making Marissa feel light-headed.

"Did your father really breed horses?" he asked her presently.

"Yes, of course." She laughed. "Did you think I had made it up?" They came to a stretch of open land and she proceeded to demonstrate her ability, taking him by surprise. She heard his exclamation and very soon the thunder of hooves as he caught up with her.

"I believe you!" he cried, laughing at her. "Is there no end to your accomplishments?"

"Oh, I am not so special."

"That," he said provocatively, "is a matter of opinion. When does the season end at the Opera House?"

"At the end of July, I think. There is to be a Royal Command on the Thursday of the final week in June."

"You are honored indeed!"

"It is not just for me," she said, blushing. "The Prince Regent has been pleased to invite me several times to sing for him, I know. And I am to go to his Brighton Pavilion in August to entertain his guests, but the Command is for all the company!"

Mr. Maxwell gave her a sanguine look. "And after July?"

"A rest, I hope." She sighed. "There are one or two concerts—one at Vauxhall Gardens. But other than that—well, I would like to get Cosmo into the country. We shall look for a house, perhaps . . ."

"You are very solicitous for Signor Pucci's well-being," he said casually.

She ignored the implication. "He has been very good to me."

He inclined his head. "And in the autumn? You are to have an opera written especially for you, I'm told . . . at the instigation of Sir Hugo Severin? One had no idea that Severin was such a patron of the Arts!"

Marissa looked at him in amused surprise. "Why, Mr. Maxwell, can it be that I detect the tiniest note of sourness in your voice?"

If she had hoped to discomfort him, she was disappointed. There was, however, an oddly austere cast to his features as she glanced at him. "Not sour, my dear, just cautionary. Sir Hugo seldom does anything without a carefully considered motive."

She wondered what there was between the two men. They were polite to one another, but beneath the surface there was something. She had once asked Celestine, who had laughed and said airily, "I did once hear of a quarrel—it was over a woman, I suppose. It almost always is!"

Since Marissa could hardly ask him, she said instead with a light laugh, "Well, you need not trouble yourself, sir, for neither do I!"

It was the only serious moment in an idyllic day.

When it became clear that the weather was to continue glorious, it was unanimously decided that they would all go for a picnic down by the river. There was a lot of laughter and a lot of outrageous flirting, and in the afternoon, the gentlemen, having discovered a pair of rowing boats kept by Mrs. Arbuthnot, magnanimously offered to take the ladies on the river. Lady Drusilla and Mrs. Arbuthnot declined the honor, but the rest expressed themselves as more than willing.

"Not for anything would we miss such a treat!" cried Celestine.

"Indeed, no!" Marissa agreed. "Rupert, I can quite visualize in command of the oars, but Lord Ravensdale and Mr. Maxwell . . . !" They both went off into whoops of laughter, in which the Baroness quickly joined.

For answer, Mr. Maxwell divested himself of his coat with an air of ironic superiority, and laid it, carefully folded upon the bank.

"I cannot vouch for his lordship," he said dryly. "But I will have you know that my years at Oxford were not entirely wasted upon study."

Rupert chuckled. "Now you've done it! Touched upon his pride, don't you know!" He removed his own coat. "Come, my lord—are you game to join the sport?"

Lord Ravensdale opened sleepy eyes. "Must I?" he complained, but unfurled his long legs, obedient to his beloved's added entreaty. He proved to be much more efficient than he looked and Mr. Maxwell's technique was masterly. Thus most of the afternoon passed and they returned at last to find the two remaining ladies fast asleep and snoring gently beneath the shade of a willow tree. By evening they were all satiated with fresh air and a surfeit of pleasure; Marissa could not remember when she had enjoyed herself half so well, and it showed.

Mrs. Arbuthnot's *chef de cuisine* prepared a superb dinner which they ate in a small paneled dining room with the windows wide open to the evening air. When the ladies left the gentlemen to their port, they repaired to the French saloon and Lady Drusilla drifted across to the spinet in the corner and began to play, continuing to do so when the gentlemen rejoined them. For a while they all sat in a pleasantly relaxed fashion, listening and talking, Marissa contributing little, but utterly content, so much so that even the presence of Mr. Maxwell at her side seemed right; the smile he turned upon her occasionally as they spoke had a gentleness and an intimacy that made her feel cherished. He never sought to overstep the boundaries of what was fitting and she went to bed that night convinced that she had misjudged him and was prey to unsettling dreams.

The following day, the last of their visit, passed in much the same way, except that during the course of the evening the Baroness asked very prettily whether they might not dance.

"The easiest thing in the world, m'dear!" Mrs. Arbuthnot, resplendent in a kaftan presented to her by a sultan of some obscure eastern state, was up from her chair on the instant and pealing on the bell to summon Watts, requiring him when he arrived to send in a pair of footmen to turn back the rug. This accomplished, Lady Drusilla announced herself more than content to play for them. With only three couples, the choice was limited to simple country dance steps and the waltz, the latter being by far the most popular, and this time Mr. Maxwell showed no reluctance to dance.

He moved every bit as well as Marissa had anticipated, and long before they had completed one circle of the room, she had surrendered herself with a reckless abandon to a sensation that was more like floating than dancing. At first neither spoke; for her part, Marissa had no wish to destroy a moment of sheer perfection.

"We are good together, you and I," he murmured, endorsing her unspoken thoughts.

"Oh, yes!" she agreed dreamily.

His laugh was soft. "But then you have known how it would be, just as I have, from the very first moment we met."

She stumbled, lost her step and was intimately held and set right. "No," she said. "You mustn't say such things!"

"So be it," he agreed, but with a look that made nonsense of the words.

Marissa went to enormous pains from that time to avoid being alone with him and he, humoring her, made no attempt to press her. But with so few of them, it was inevitable that, short of pleading a sudden indisposition which her pride would not permit, or the possibility that Lady Drusilla might tire of playing for them, her reprieve could not last forever.

"It won't work, you know," he said, whirling her around with expert precision. Through the fineness of the *mousseline de soie* his hand seemed to scorch her back.

"I don't know what you mean," she said valiantly .

"Running away. Sooner or later, you'll have to give in."

There was an unbearable tightness in her throat. "Give in?"

"'*Come live with me and be my love. And we will all the pleasures prove . . .*'" The words were the merest whisper, but in her agitation it seemed as though he had shouted it to the room. Heedless of what the others might think, she pulled away from him and ran toward the open window, through and down the terrace steps, and across the lawns, not stopping until she was almost at the stream.

It was a perfect night; a full moon and the air drenched with the scent of roses. The lightest of breezes shivered along a row of graceful larches, and she, too, shivered though her cheeks burned. So short a time ago she had known exactly what she wanted from life, had been so sure of her reasons. Now, her senses were in a turmoil.

There had been no sound, yet she knew he had followed her. His nearness brought a wild tingling to her blood that made nonsense of all her fine ideals. He dropped a light wrap across her shoulders, his hands folding it around her, drawing her back against him. So sure of himself!

"Can't have you risking a chill," he murmured against her hair. "Bad for the voice."

"Mr. Maxwell, please let me go!"

"Gervase," he corrected her with amused tenderness, and drew her closer.

"You aren't being fair!" she protested.

"Hush," His voice seduced her with its deep soft resonance. "Don't spoil a lovely light with argument. '*In such a night stood Dido with a willow in her hand upon the wild sea bank, and sighed her love to come again to Carthage.*'" Oh, it really wasn't fair of him to quote her favorite romantic verse at her!

If I don't resist, he will release me, she told herself, knowing that she didn't want to be released—ever. She clung to reason and strove to keep her tone light.

"You are in a vastly poetic mood tonight, sir, but

your themes quarrel with one another, for this one I know is from *The Merchant of Venice!* And Lorenzo, for all that he was feckless, *did* marry his Jessica!"

"Oh, marriage!" He brushed aside her argument as though it were of little moment. "I leave all that nonsense to the likes of Perry."

To Marissa, already in a state of heighted sensitivity, on the very brink of throwing aside all inhibitions and counting the world well lost for love, his offhandedness appeared as a bitter affront, seeming to strip her of any true worth as comprehensively as if he had ripped the dress from her back. A need to hold to her self-respect made her swallow on the anger and disappointment, and that something else which would not be defined, but which lay like an aching void in her chest.

"You think marriage nonsense?" She was amazed that her voice could sound so normal.

"I do. I also think it dull and boring, and designed specifically to sound the death knell of all passion! People should marry for expediency, but not for love." He attempted to draw her closer, found his efforts resisted and fell to coaxing. "Come, *carissima mia,* the time for teasing is over. You are a splendid actress, but you don't really want to fight me! Your eyes have betrayed you a hundred times these past two days, so cry 'Pax' and let us enjoy what is left of the night. You know that we belong together." His lips were punctuating the words, moving ever more persuasively into the curve of her neck. His hands were at her shoulders; something shimmered before her eyes and in a moment lay cold against her skin.

Marissa put up a hand to touch it—a collar of diamonds? Her breath caught and she turned resolutely in his arms, leaning back so that she might look up into his face.

"Are you attempting to buy me, Mr. Maxwell?"

There was that now familiar quizzical arch of the eyebrow. "Gervase," he prompted again. "And no, you absurd girl, I am not buying you! The necklace is but a token of how gloriously, ecstatically happy I mean you to be."

"How thoughtful of you to come prepared," she said politely. And then, a little disgusted with herself as the full impact of his words struck her: "Were you really *so* sure of me?"

"Sure enough," he admitted with what seemed odious complacence.

Night masked the shaming tide of color that swept her face. "I am having a most instructive evening, am I not? A step-by-step education in the art and stratagems of a philanderer. *Be prepared* will be your guiding maxim, I daresay? It is a very simple and convenient philosophy . . . I applaud you for it! No, really, I do! No young lady in her right mind should be able to resist such a combination of persuasions . . . soft words and the very solid reality of diamonds together with the not inconsiderable cache of being recognized as the mistress of such a true gentleman of quality!"

She saw his teeth gleam in the darkness. "I had a notion you'd be a bad loser! But we'll fight later. I don't want to argue with you now!"

So he refused to take her seriously? Well, she would make him listen. "Do you have a sister, Mr. Maxwell?"

A certain good-natured exasperation was beginning to show. "No, I do not. Come, my exceedingly prickly love, you are being silly and we are wasting precious moments!"

"But if you had?" she persisted. "How would you react if someone were to offer *her* 'carte blanche'? Or"—in a wild desire to inflict the same hurt upon him that she was feeling, she searched for a more telling argument and found one. "Or Lady Kitty, perhaps?"

His face was etched like marble in the moonlight; his voice, the voice of a stranger. "We will leave Lady Kitty's name out of this curious little debate, if you please . . ."

"Oh, by all means!" So Perry had been right about his tendre for Lady Kitty! Marissa's stifled laugh had little of mirth in it. "Heaven forbid that we should sully the name of a virtuous woman! And anyway, it no longer matters for my question is answered. Do you have any idea, I wonder, how insulting that answer appears? You assume, as do most people, that because I work in the theater I cannot possibly be virtuous and am consequently any man's for the taking, allowing that he has a persuasive tongue and wealth enough to tempt me. I am thus condemned without ever a word being spoken!"

"Condemned?" His voice was heavy with irony. His arms remained around her, only now they confined her like bands of steel. "My dear signorina, I fear your preoccupation with the dramatic arts has somewhat colored your thinking. You have been treated exactly as your behavior has dictated—and as for Society, I would say that you have been accepted with more generosity than is usually accorded to . . ." He paused.

"Why do you hesitate?" Marissa flung the words at him. "To my kind of woman. Is that not it? You have been more than forthright so far—pray do not boggle at plain speaking now! You are quite right, of course. As a singer I am much sought after!" Her irony outrivaled his. "The Prince Regent even invites me to Carlton House to sing for his friends—high-born gentlemen all! Well, you see me there—do you call that acceptance? The extravagant compliments masking subtle innuendos . . . the costly presents . . .

the crude attempts at flirtation! Not all, of course. Some are simply kind—the Prince, for all his reputation, has never attempted to overstep the bounds of good manners. But, for the rest—do you know how it feels to be accorded that kind of civility? Sometimes I can even see the speculation behind their eyes. 'Will she—won't she.' But no doubt you will consider such an attitude no more or less than my *behavior* merits?" She knew she was being childish, but once begun, she couldn't stop. "And the wives and mothers of these splendid gentlemen are constantly pressing me to attend musical soirees and are most gracious in their patronage, but they do not invite me to their *ton* parties."

"Ha! So it is dull respectability you really crave! How disappointing." His voice was cutting, now. "Well, you will certainly find dullness if you marry Perry; I daresay in time you may even achieve a degree of respectability, if you don't die of boredom first!"

"Don't sneer at Perry!" she cried. "He, at least, has never made me feel cheap, or tried to ... to ..."

"*Take advantage* is, I think, the phrase you are seeking," he said helpfully. "And he will, of course, one day be the Earl of Weare!"

"Is that how you regard me?" Her eyes were luminous with a film of unshed tears that blotted out his image. "Then it is well to know now, for it proves the madness of supposing that there can ever be anything between us!"

Gervase was angry; more, he was outraged. How dare she try to put *him* in the wrong! He was used to conducting his affairs with charm, with an easy amiability; never, until now, had any woman suggested that he had behaved less than handsomely toward her. He was about to tell her so when a tear, hovering tremulously on her lower lashes, was blinked away impatiently and rolled unheeded down her cheek. It had a curious effect on him, turning his indignation without warning to a kind of tender exasperation. He pulled her close.

"But what a sweet madness it would be!" he said softly.

Marissa struggled, but not for long; with ignominious ease she surrendered herself to his kiss, tasting the salt of her own tears in its questing thoroughness; light-headed, irrational—she felt deprived when he at last released her.

"Can Perry make you feel like that?" he murmured against her hair.

She knew she ought to say something, but her mouth would not behave. It was his laugh, low and exultant, that brought her sharply back to earth.

"Perhaps not." The words were forced out. "But it changes nothing."

She stepped away from him, head high, and he let her go.

"You'll come to me yet," he called after her.

She looked back briefly, challenging once more. "As your wife, Mr. Maxwell?"

"I think not." His smile was the merest glimmer. "You would have much more fun as my mistress!"

"And when you tire of me?" Her voice was much firmer now. "Will you then find some obliging Austrian count to take *me* off your hands?"

The words floated back to Gervase across the serene perfection of the moonlit lawns. At his feet a frog croaked, mocking him.

"Damn!" he said aloud. "Oh, damn, damn, damn!"

Chapter 7

Marissa returned to London, apparently in the highest of spirits and eager to resume her engagements. Only those closest to her observed a brittle edge to her gaiety and wondered at it, and of these, only Maria knew what it cost her to preserve such a front.

Maria would not quickly forget that last evening when the signorina had come running up to her room wearing around her neck a most beautiful glittering necklace of diamonds—or her almost hysterical distress upon beholding the maid's incoherent admiration and then her own image in the mirror; and when frantic struggles to release the clasp were unsuccessful, her demands that she, Maria, should accomplish this task.

Just for a few seconds, she had been privileged to hold the precious object in her hand—and then it was snatched from her and tied, with scant respect for its worth in a handkerchief, and Maria was charged to deliver it, together with a note, penned hastily and in a shaking hand, to Mr. Maxwell's room. The signorina had shed copious tears that night, but had extracted from Maria a solemn oath that she would never, under any circumstances, reveal what had happened; and the young girl, deeply impressionable and aware of some great, unrevealed heartbreak in her mistress's tragic demeanor, had sworn passionately that even were they to cut out her tongue, no word should ever pass her lips. It had been a little disconcerting upon the following morning to find her mistress apparently quite recovered, but there were moments when the mask had slipped a little and she had realized how brave a countenance the signorina was showing to the world. Knowing this, she was able to resist successfully even the superior inquisitorial powers of Signora Tortinallo, until that lady was finally obliged to abandon the interrogation.

The maid's stubbornness remained a continuing source of aggravation to the signora, however, who was convinced that whatever ailed her charge, it was in some way connected with that rose, the mysterious delivery of which had ceased abruptly on the day of Marissa's departure to Chiswick and had not been resumed. This much was confirmed to her when a small comment about the rose brought a pallor to Marissa's cheek sufficient to warn her to proceed no further.

Celestine was likewise overcome with curiosity. She was naturally distressed that two of her dearest friends had quarreled, for the more Gervase wore his polite face that discouraged questions, and protested that she had too-fertile an imagination; and the more Marissa laughed aloud at the merest suggestion that there might ever have been sufficient between Mr. Maxwell and herself to provoke a quarrel—"We simply enjoyed a weekend in one another's company, thrown together as we were!"—the more convinced did she become that both had a great deal to conceal. Also she found it difficult to equate their lighthearted dismissal of her concern with the odd circumstances of that last night at Chiswick when they had both disappeared into the garden and only Gervase had returned, tendering Marissa's apologies for her sudden tiredness and looking, in spite of his attempts to appear otherwise, tight-lipped, a little drawn, and quite lacking his usual élan.

However, on the face of it, once back in Town there seemed little evidence to support her theories. Marissa had never been in better voice and with any number of engagements to fulfill, seemed content and without a moment to spare, while Gervase was soon to be seen regularly with an ethereal, silver-haired vision upon his arm, a vision blessed with voluptuous curves and an enchanting lisp.

"Damned if I know where he finds 'em!" Rupert observed with a twinge of envy. "No Paphians of that order ever fell into my lap!"

"Thank you, *chéri!*" Celestine made a little *moue*.

"Begging your pardon, m'dear." Rupert grinned. "Delectable, you undoubtedly are—incomparable, even, but a Paphian you ain't! Wouldn't be invited to Lady Chess's ball an' you were, of course!" he said as an after-thought, reminding her of that last and most glittering event of the Season, so soon to be held.

"I just wish it might have been Marissa!" Celestine sighed.

"Eh?" Rupert followed her eyes which were upon Gervase, whose phaeton was at that moment approaching them down Park Lane, and more particularly upon his ravishing companion. "Yes, well—not much use setting your hopes in that direction, I fear. Pity! Seen our little signorina in Severin's company once or twice of late . . . his connections with that musician chappie, I suppose. Still"—Rupert shook his head, his pleasant features wrinkled with thought—"I don't like it above half. Never thought I'd say so, for I don't believe *he's* the right man for her either, but it'll be no bad thing when young Marlowe gets back to Town!"

The carriages had by now drawn level and Rupert

raised his hat with a flourish, his eyes twinkling appreciatively, as Miss Perdita Wellam dressed all in white (just like a bride! muttered Celestine unkindly) lifted fluttering lashes to reveal eyes of the deepest blue to smile archly at him, and a little less so at Celestine.

"Major Egerton—madame, how twuly delightful to meet you! And just when we were speaking of you. Do you go to the Command Performance on Thursday next? I have been twying to persuade this naughty man to take me, but he will not make up his mind!"

She tapped Gervase playfully with her furled parasol and Celestine, her delicate eyebrows raised in amusement, looked in vain for some reaction on his part. He continued to look bland, but since Gervase was not a man to suffer fools, even divinely pretty fools, indefinitely, she was confident that Miss Wellam's more obvious assets would not long compensate for the more irritating tendencies in her nature. This was born out as the breathy voice prattled on.

"I wondered if we might not make up a small party for the occasion?"

"An excellent notion, ma'am," said Rupert heartily. "And supper afterward perhaps, at Gunter's. Eh?"

Miss Wellam was overjoyed and went on about it at great length, but Celestine thought that Gervase looked less than pleased.

Marissa could hardly fail to be made aware of Mr. Maxwell's new conquest; it was so much discussed. She could only be thankful that their brief affair had been played out in comparative obscurity; since neither of them out of sheer pride would stoop to avoid those places where they would most likely meet, it was inevitable that they must soon come face to face and what a time the rumor-mongers would have if they knew. That it happened at Mrs. Arbuthnot's house was but an added twist in the wound for Marissa. She arrived with Sir Hugo and found Mrs. Arbuthnot anxious to draw her on one side.

"I wonder, Sir Hugo . . . would you mind if I just had a private word with Signorina Merrilli? I'll not keep her above a moment."

He bowed, looked a trifle put out, but sauntered away to be absorbed presently into a group of acquaintances, while the good lady launched into speech in her usual blunt fashion.

". . . I could see how things were between you that weekend. I've been a bit troubled in my mind about it—well, I like things straightforward, as you know. I'm not one for secrets and surprises and the like! But that Gervase Maxwell has quite a way with him"—she chuckled—"and in the event it seemed he was right, except that I suspicioned something went wrong on that last evening."

Marissa opened her mouth to speak.

"No, I don't want to know. It's none of my business, but the thing is, my dear Marissa, I'd not like you to be hurt, so I thought you should know that he's here tonight, and he's not alone, so if you'd sooner not stay . . ."

"My dear friend!" Marissa managed a convincing laugh. "I beg you will set your mind at ease. I do know about Miss Wellam, and can meet her if I must without rancor. What happened to us was a moment of fleeting madness, born of . . . oh, of propinquity; of summer magic and moonshine! And as such, you know it could never have survived reality!"

Mrs. Arbuthnot looked less than convinced. "Are you telling me that you don't care?"

Such forthrightness was disconcerting. Marissa prevaricated. "I am saying that I do not repine over lost causes. Mr. Maxwell is your friend, as I trust I am, also. A tiresome thing it would be an you were obliged to juggle us, like a pantomime clown with a handful of oranges, lest we should collide with one another! If he is content, so am I." A touch of defiance, here. "We are civilized beings, after all, and can, I hope, behave as such when we meet."

It was very much in this same mood of defiance, with head proudly held on slender neck and knowing she looked well in her embroidered Venetian dress, that she was presently able to face the frail creature in spangled gauze who hung so possessively on Mr. Maxwell's arm—a naiadlike figure whose slip (surely her only other garment) must have been well damped in order to make it cling in such a tantalizing way to her curves (an uncharitable assessment, but one which gave Marissa immense satisfaction). It even enabled her to bear with reasonable equanimity the sight of the delicate circlet of diamonds around Miss Wellam's throat.

Gervase had watched her sweep toward them, her every movement a joy to behold, her flair for the dramatic apparent in the confidence of her approach. Yet he knew her so well that he could pierce that bright smile to glimpse the hurt this meeting was inflicting upon her. He compared her with the inoffensively silly child at his side, and in every respect found Perdita Wellam wanting. It was not Perdita's fault; he had taken her up as a balm to his pride and had regretted it almost from the first moment.

But she was proving so confoundedly tenacious that he feared it would be the devil's own work to shift her—and would cost him dear. Even so, one glimmer of encouragement from Marissa and shift her he would no matter what the cost. With this thought uppermost he caught Marissa's eye and found her as unyielding as ever. The old exasperation rose in him. How dare she balk him with her stubbornness when everything between them might be so perfect! He'd be damned if he would make things easy for her. He accomplished the introductions with practiced ease, and instead of making polite conversation, fell unhelpfully silent.

Marissa, refusing to be discomposed, rose to the occasion, drew a deep breath, and said without a tremor, "You outshine us all, tonight, Miss Wellam. Mr. Maxwell is indeed a fortunate man!" A complacent little giggle, an upward fluttering of eyelashes greeted this encomium. Marissa looked with interest to see how it was received, but could discern little change in his bland expression. She continued. "I hope you will not mind if I remark upon your necklace? How delightfully it becomes you! I noticed it most particularly, for strangely enough I very nearly acquired a very similar one myself quite recently."

She sensed rather than saw the slight tensing of Mr. Maxwell's elegant figure and exulted that she had moved him to some reaction at last.

"Gervase gave it to me," cooed Miss Wellam, unaware of anything amiss. She stroked the necklace with possessive fingers. "If yours was half so pwetty, I am sure I don't know how you were able to wesist it!"

Marissa looked Mr. Maxwell full in the eye and met a dark, derisive challenge.

"It was not easy," she said. "But in the end, you see, the price was too high."

His expression did not alter, yet she was left in no doubt that he could have wrung her neck with great pleasure. With a sense of satisfaction, she begged to be excused as Sir Hugo would be wondering where she had got to, a comment calculated to add a final inflammatory thrust. As they parted, he contrived to brush close to her.

"Vixen!" he murmured with relish.

Her laugh was a triumphant trill of mockery.

The following day Perry returned to London, a fact which did not please Sir Hugo. He had taken full advantage of Lord Marlowe's absence, and of his own growing involvement in Marissa's professional life, to advance himself in her estimation. Marissa's feelings about him were ambivalent—he could indeed be a most entertaining and considerate companion, though his wit on occasions had too biting an edge to please her, but his interest in her career was flattering, and this together with a general concern for her well-being often expressed in Signor Pucci's hearing, had made him a frequent and a welcome visitor in Arlington Street. Toward Signora Tortinallo he was all graciousness, and although she was not a woman to be bought with sweet words, she allowed him to be a fine discerning gentleman. He was not, however, the sender of the roses—of that she was sure. And perhaps that was no bad thing. Such quixotic behavior was not to be relied upon!

Perry confessed to Marissa that he had not mentioned any word of his regard for her, or its eventual outcome, to his parents.

"Mama was so low in spirits," he said a little sheepishly, "And Kitty who was there also persuaded me that it would be the worst possible of times . . . because of Papa, you know . . . he can be jolly stiff-rumped when he gets some maggot in his head! But Kitty likes you enormously!" he added as though in mitigation. "She has promised faithfully that she will ask you to her very next assembly."

"Oh, Perry!" Marissa, made sensitive by recent experiences, was sharp. "Do be realistic! You cannot force your sister into such a position and there is no reason why you should. The last thing I would wish is to cause any rift between you and your family."

"What nonsense! It was Kitty's own idea. Besides, you are now grown so famous that I dare swear there ain't anywhere you mightn't go if you chose!" Perry's face lit up as a particular thought struck him. "I have it! You can come with me to Lady Chessborough's ball ..."

"Oh, no, Perry! That is flying too high, altogether ..."

"Fustian!" he exclaimed. "It's a famous idea! The great thing is, you see, that it is to be masked, and if you wear a domino and leave before the unmasking, the high-nosed old trout will be none the wiser. Lord, though, I'd give a monkey to see her face if she knew!"

Marissa's heart sank. Did he, she wondered, realize that with every word he uttered he was confirming the essential difference between them—even now? Yet, why should she not go—and stay? Make the *ton* accept her as an equal?

"Very well," she said on impulse. "I will come with you."

Perry was so puffed up with his idea that it quite took precedence over the disquieting intelligence which he had meant to bring up, about her seeing so much of Severin.

Instead he impressed upon Marissa the necessity for secrecy in making their plans. His boyish enthusiasm amused her and she refused to trouble her head over the possible consequences. There were more important issues to fill her mind, not the least of these being the Command Performance, rehearsals for which seemed to be increasingly dominated by temperament. Madame Brunel saw difficulties and imagined slights at every turn. Relations between her and Tia Giannina deteriorated rapidly into a tirade of insults, culminating in a showdown one evening just before a performance of *Le Nozze di Figaro* when Marissa arrived at the theater to find all in uproar.

The door to her dressing room stood open, the limited space within crammed to overflowing with an excited, colorful crowd—dancers, opera chorus, scene-

101

setters, all seemingly talking at once, and somewhere at the center of it all, the upraised tones of Madame Brunel and Tia Giannina. Mr. Ebers, the theater's manager, stood on the outer fringe looking hot and flustered and not a little annoyed. He saw Marissa and hurried toward her.

"Signorina—at last! Now perhaps we can resolve this most unprecedented situation!"

"Why, Mr. Ebers! Whatever is wrong?"

A large handkerchief was produced to wipe away beads of perspiration. "You may well ask, signorina. I am not a stranger to the artistic temperament—one can scarcely avoid it in this business! But this! And in one hour the opera must go on!"

"Quite so, Mr. Ebers, but what *has* happened?"

"My dear lady, did I not tell you?" A flourish of the handkerchief. "You see how distraught I am become? It is a boy—a thief, caught *in flagrante delicto*, as one might say. And your Signora Tortinallo will permit nothing to be done about him without your presence!"

"*Oh, Dio!*" Marissa began to squeeze her way through the crowd who made room amiably when they saw who it was. Eager voices were quick to enlighten her.

"A boy has been caught, signorina . . ."

". . . regular rum dab . . ."

"Madame Brunel's had this flash cove watching us all . . ."

Someone mimicked Madame's voice with cruel accuracy. "The imputations against certain persons here having become unsupportable . . ."

Marissa had by now reached the place beneath the swaying lamp where a youth stood quiescent between a burly man across whose catskin waistcoat a gold chain was ostentatiously displayed, and their own stage-door keeper. The boy was being harangued by

102

Madame Brunel, who in turn was being snapped at by Signora Tortinallo; occasionally the boy gave back as good as he got.

Signora Tortinallo raised her head, and beholding Marissa, demanded silence. Her booming delivery stopped all argument immediately. An air of expectancy replaced it.

Marissa stood a moment looking at the youth. He was a little older than she had supposed—perhaps fifteen years, perhaps more, stick-thin and shabbily, but not badly, dressed in what could well be some kind of livery. His long thin features displayed a jaunty arrogance in the face of his predicament that found in her a sympathetic echo, and the bright blue eyes looking into hers held a curious mixture of defiance and adoration.

"What is your name?"

"Elijah, miss."

She kept her countenance with difficulty. "Elijah ... what?"

"Briggs, miss." He half grinned.

A titter ran round the room. Madame grew restive. "His name is of no account. See?" She pointed to the table where a silver shoe buckle and a handkerchief lay. "These he had in his hand when he was caught! The constable must be summoned, and the criminal handed in charge. It should even now be accomplished!" She shot a venomous glance at the signora. "How I am to perform after such an upset only the Good God knows!"

"It is so with all who meddle where they have no business!" declared her adversary undaunted. "May I suggest that Madame returns to her quarters in the instant, there to attempt the near impossibility of restoring the ravages wrought by her own ill temper?"

"Tia Giannina!" Marissa's voice was sharp, her look reproachful. "Madame"—she turned to the distraught singer—"I am most grateful to you for bringing this matter to my notice, but now"—she raised her voice to include them all—"I think it would be for the best if everyone were to leave the rest to me. The time grows short and if we are to give a performance . . ."

In an atmosphere of anticlimax, the room began to empty. Madame was led, still complaining, to the door.

"My honor demanded that the culprit be discovered. This, at least, the signorina will allow?"

"Yes, yes. But now, the performance . . ."

Marissa closed the door behind her with a sigh and turned to find the remaining tableau unchanged—the youth still flanked by his joint apprehenders—and Tia Giannina dwarfing the lot of them. The doorkeeper was dispatched back to his duties, which left the burly man.

"The matter of the constable, ma'am—if I may make so bold?"

She regarded him pensively, well aware that the youth for all his jauntiness, was hanging on her answer.

"Mr. . . . ?"

"Thomkins, ma'am—Joshua Thomkins." The catskin waistcoat threatened to burst its buttons. "You'll be wanting this young hang-gallows . taken in charge, ma'am, I've no doubt?"

Marissa turned to meet the bright blue gaze. "Well, Elijah? Am I to hand you over to the constable?"

"Not if you're one-half the angel as you appears to your ardent admirers up there in the gallery of a night, miss!"

"Oh-ho! This one has a smooth way with him!" scoffed Tia Giannina. "Do not listen, signorina . . . I have heard such silver-tongued rogues many times! He will insinuate himself into your graces and rob you even as he lulls you with sweet words!"

"That's a bleedin' lie!"

"You hold your language afor a lady, my lad, if you don't want a touch of the home-brewed!" advised Mr. Thomkins.

The boy subsided into a sullen silence.

"Why did you take my things, Elijah?" Marissa asked out of sheer curiosity. "This isn't the first time, is it?" He shrugged. "And why such oddments? There were many more valuable items you might have stolen."

He shuffled his feet and muttered. "Won't tell that to no one but you, miss."

Marissa sighed, considered the advancing time, and made up her mind. She pressed a coin into Mr. Thomkins's hand. "Thank you," she said simply. "You have been most helpful, but I don't believe this is a matter for the constable. Good night, Mr. Thomkins."

He stared, shook his head at Elijah, and sniffed. "Well, you've landed in clover and no mistake, young cully! I only hope as the young lady don't have call to regret her generosity!" Upon which note he bowed and departed.

"I think you are crazed in the head!" said the signora flatly, and began to lay out her costume.

"Well, Elijah?"

He turned bright red and jerked his head in the signora's direction. Marissa gave him a wry look and cajoled Tia Giannina into leaving them for two minutes. Lapsing into Italian, she pointed out the boy's acute embarrassment. "I think he wishes to confess to an acute infatuation and is afraid you will ridicule him . . ." Tia Giannina grunted and grumbled about murderers, but she went, exhorting Marissa to remember the time.

The two were left alone, an oddly assorted pair—the elegant opera singer and the out-at-elbows youth. Marissa smiled encouragingly and put him at ease, busied herself in stripping off her gloves and untying the ribbons of her bonnet, removing it and setting it aside.

"I really do have very little time to spare just now," she explained. "You won't mind if I make a start?"

"N-no, miss. I shouldn't ought to be here, really, I know!" He shuffled. "I'm sorry . . . about taking them things. It weren't stealing . . . not culling, proper, if you take my meaning . . ."

"Of course not," she said in a matter-of-fact way. "More in the nature of a keepsake, perhaps?" He grinned with a touch of his old jauntiness. "I am most flattered. Do you frequent the gallery often?"

"The old tr——" He cleared his throat. "The lady I worked for, was a regular one for the opera, used to attend the theater regular—and being mortal afraid of footpads and the like, she would have me along of the coachman and the groom as extra protection, if you please! Much good I'd be against footpads!" Elijah looked down at his skinny frame and the thought seemed to amuse him.

"Anyhow, that's how I came to be in the gallery. I'd never been to a theater, d'ye see, let alone such a fine grand place, and being a great believer in takin' any advantage as is offered, I thought why not, it'll pass the time! And then I saw you, miss, and what with the surroundings and everything, it was like magic!—like all the sunshine and the warmth and color of a summer's day was in your eyes that first night! It was in your voice too, in every movement . . . Stripe me, I'd never seen anything so beautiful in all my days!"

Elijah was quite carried away by his own eloquence and Marissa, listening to the stumbling words, found his naive sincerity more moving than all the compliments she was used to receive.

"You couldn't've kept me away after that!" He shuffled self-consciously. "Them things I took—I never meant to steal them, y'know, straight I didn't! It was just that I wanted something . . . any little thing as you'd worn, or touched, even, as a kind of keepsake. Only it got to be a habit, you see? The laugh is"—he didn't sound in the least amused—"tonight would likely have been the last time. Old Mrs. B. turned her toes up last week . . ."

"Turned her toes?" Marissa asked.

"Snuffed her candle!" he further elaborated; and when she still looked puzzled, "Took and died, miss. And, like as not, her son won't keep the house, so that be the end of my theater-going for a bit."

"But what will you do?"

Elijah shrugged, cheerfully philosophic. "Something'll turn up. It allus does." He half raised his clasped hands in a gesture toward the door and grinned. "That old foreign besom'll be having ten fits out there! I'd best be off, anyhow, if it's all right with you miss, else I'll miss me place in the gallery queue! Oh, and about them things . . ." He swallowed, rather as though the words were choking him. "I still have them all there, in a box, if you want them back . . ."

"No, oh, no! I wouldn't hear of it!" cried Marissa. "But you are right—I *must* dress now, at once!" She couldn't bear to dismiss him so summarily. As he gave a quaint courtly bow and turned to the door, she said, "Wait! Elijah, if you can't find work, come to see me in Arlington Street—" She hastily scribbled the address on a slip of paper and thrust it at him. "I might be able to help. Now, go!"

"*Yes, miss!*" He passed Signora Tortinallo in the doorway, his former jauntiness very much in evidence as he bade her good evening. Marissa was bustled out of her dress and into her costume at an alarming rate. "A soft heart is very well, but that boy will be as a stone about your neck! See if I am not right! Foreign besom, indeed!"

Chapter 8

As the day of Lady Chessborough's ball drew nearer, Marissa found herself prey to all the misgivings which had been thrust resolutely to the back of her mind from the moment she had ordered her domino from one of London's most exclusive modistes. Not that one could easily forget about the ball, for everyone was talking about it.

"So tiresome, *chérie.*" Celestine pouted charmingly. "One is obliged to arrive almost embarrassingly early or face the prospect of having to walk for a great distance in order to arrive at all! Last year, the Square was blocked solidly with carriages; the constables and link-boys and coachmen almost coming to blows, as each was determined to press their least advantage, and the streets surrounding the Square were in little better case! One can only pray for a fine night!" She sighed deeply.

"You do not sound as though you find much pleasure in it," Marissa said. "So why do you go?"

"But, my dear, everyone goes!" And then, seeing Marissa's expression and realizing how tactless were her words, "That is, all of the *haut ton*, of course! And you know how much I enjoy to discompose them with my presence!"

Nothing could have been more surely guaranteed to bolster Marissa's faltering courage; Celestine's reasoning was so very much in sympathy with her own that had she not promised Perry, she might very easily have confided her intention there and then. As it was, she kept her counsel until the very morning of the ball when the large bandbox bearing Madame Claudine's monogram and tied with the distinctive striped ribbons was carried up to her room where it was received with reverence by Maria.

By the time news of its delivery had brought Signora Tortinallo panting onto the scene, mistress and maid were knee-deep in snowy drifts of tissue paper and Marissa was lifting aloft a silken domino of deepest pink, holding it against herself and swaying in a few experimental movements.

Maria sighed. "Ah, signorina! Such a color! How it glows, like a jewel!"

"What is this?" demanded the signora in awful tones, annoyed that she should have been kept in ignorance of such happenings.

Marissa sighed dreamily. "It is a domino, Tia Giannina."

"Am I blind? Of course it is a domino!" Suddenly aware of Maria's interested gaze, Signora Tortinallo packed her off about her business, having first exhorted her to gather up the tissue paper and remove it, together with the bandbox.

"Oh, wait!" cried Marissa, throwing the gown upon the bed to delve once more among the tissue, emerging in triumph dangling from her fingers an elaborate mask in the same shade of deep rose pink with delicate silver-tipped wings sweeping up and away at the outer edges. "There! Is this not beautiful?"

"Exquisite," agreed the older woman dryly. "But I ask myself why you would need such an elaborate disguise?"

"That is simple. One cannot go to a masquerade ball without a mask."

"Naturally, one appreciates such reasoning. And

this ball you speak of—how is it that I know nothing of it?"

Why did Tia Giannina have to be so inquisitive? Marissa sat down before the mirror to try on the mask. It was exactly right, covering sufficient of her face to make recognition difficult. She said airily, "I thought I had told you. It is tonight—at Lady Chessborough's."

Tia Giannina came to peer suspiciously over her shoulder; in the mirror their eyes met, Marissa's glittering defiantly, very glad that the mask so efficiently hid her blushes.

"The Lady Chessborough invites you to her ball?"

"And why should she not?" Marissa sprang up and donned the domino, drawing the hood well forward to conceal her hair. "There!" She swirled around. "The perfect masquerader!"

"This is what troubles me!" muttered the old lady darkly.

To Marissa's surprise and relief, Cosmo proved rather easier to deceive. Beyond an initial disappointment upon learning that she was to go with Lord Marlowe rather than Sir Hugo or Mr. Maxwell, he seemed content to admire her appearance with every degree of partiality, prophesying that she would grace any ball, masquerade or otherwise, by her mere presence.

With the plans for the new opera now well underway, Signor Pucci had grown increasingly preoccupied; it was for him the fulfillment of a dream and he had become obsessed with insuring that it would be a *succès fou*. Marissa was afraid that he was driving himself too hard and she knew that Tia Giannina worried too. She mentioned her fears to Sir Hugo,

"My dear young lady," drawled Sir Hugo. "Only tell me how I may prevent him and I will gladly do

111

so. You must know that I am your willing slave in all things and live only to prove it to you."

She wished he wouldn't say such things. He never did so in Cosmo's hearing. Only when Marissa was alone with him did she sense a growing possessiveness in his manner, a certain veiled hunger in his eyes which caused her heart to beat a trifle unsteadily.

Gervase had warned her about Sir Hugo, of course, though what right he had to question the motives of others when his own conduct was so devious, selfish, and utterly unprincipled she couldn't imagine! How heartily glad she was that he had not succeeded in swaying her with his soft words and insidious charm! If only she might cure herself of the stupid compulsion to search every room she entered for a sight of his tall distinguished figure, she was confident of being able to meet him eventually without that awful hollowing in her chest, or the wholly unbidden urge which made her want to scratch poor Miss Wellam's eyes out every time she simpered up at him.

Celestine, who missed very little, had also noticed Sir Hugo's growing interest. Concern for her friend caused her to make casual reference to it.

"Yes, I know, but what am I to do when Cosmo has come to rely upon him so heavily?" Marissa sighed. "At first it seemed such a splendid thing that he was doing for me—I suppose I was even a little flattered that he should put himself out to advance my career. And, you know, in spite of his sarcastic manner, he has a certain compelling air of attraction . . ."

"So has a snake," said Celestine with alarming frankness. "For me there is a coldness in Sir Hugo which chills the blood. His amusement invariably derives from someone else's discomfiture. If ever he was young, which I take leave to doubt, he will have been the kind of little boy who enjoys to pull the wings off insects simply to observe what happens."

"Oh, no, you must be wrong! He is not *such* a monster! I think that I am tired and it is this which makes me prey to foolish thoughts. But perhaps I will strive harder to avoid being alone with him in the future."

Marissa's decision meant, however, that she must continue to encourage Perry's attentions for a little while longer; the thought that she was using him filled her sometimes with a sense of guilt, but there was no one else to whom she could turn, and surely if she was careful it could be done without any hurt to him.

On the night of the masquerade-ball, excitement, spiced with a heady element of risk, took hold of her from the moment she donned the rose domino and secured the strings of her mask. Nothing could destroy it, not even Tia Giannina's exaggerated sighs. The total blockage of St. James's Square was every bit as comprehensive as Celestine had prophesied and necessitated their walking for the last few hundred yards, but the night was warm, the moon shone benignly down on the grinding, swearing, whinnying melee that reverberated across the smooth kidney-shaped stones of the Square as coachmen jostled for a space in which to set down their precious cargoes. Marissa's feet in their pretty Denmark slippers hardly touched the ground as she was borne past them on Perry's arm to join the slowly moving throng which passed continuously beneath the impressive portico of Chessborough House and up the grand central staircase. All were masked and all but a very few had entered enthusiastically into the spirit of the evening and were clad in anything from dominoes to the most ambitious of historical costumes. Progress was of necessity slow, though there was to be no formal reception. "No point, really," Perry had told her, "when you ain't supposed to know who anyone is!"

There was something wonderfully liberating about a disguise, as Marissa had already discovered, and it seemed to have infected those around them. There was much laughter and some wildly inaccurate guessing of identities where these were not immediately obvious. Many admiring glances were cast her way, the ladies in particular envying her her exquisite mask, for almost everyone wore the more conventional black. It was a little like the theater, she found, and rose to the occasion almost without conscious thought, becoming the silent, enigmatic stranger, speaking only when obliged to do so and then in the husky, whispered accents of someone with only the merest smattering of English.

Thus, quite inadvertently, she made herself the focus of attention, creating an amused buzz of speculation which followed her into the ballroom.

Robert Adams's influence was everywhere to be seen at Chessborough House, but in the ballroom he had created a masterpiece—a superb illusion of light and space. Marissa, from the head of the four steps leading down to its mirror-polished floor, saw the room at its very best—not yet crowded, but with sufficient people moving about to give the scene an added warmth and brilliance. Two rows of Venetian chandeliers had been hung down the length of the room, their lusters reflecting the flickering of hundreds of candles in ever-changing hues of fiery reds and golds, of azure and greens, picked up from the rich plush hangings and the vivid colorful patchwork of dresses, ever-moving. And all this beauty was reflected again and yet again in the mirrored panels which decorated the walls.

Marissa had seen many beautiful sights in her travels, but none more exquisite than this. Her breath caught in her throat as she looked down upon it, and almost stopped completely as she saw Gervase. He was wearing formal dress comprising satin knee breeches and striped stockings, a white waistcoat, and a shirt with an unusually frivolous fall of lace ruffles to compliment his black tailed coat. These, together with a black velvet half-mask, lent him a rakish, swashbuckling air.

He was with a group of people who included a pale blue domino and a large red-haired gentleman looking much too jolly to be a monk.

"I see Kitty's here," whispered Perry, coming up behind her. "She's had that blue domino for years! And Edward too. You won't have met him, I suppose—a great gun is Edward! I must introduce you. You'll like him!"

"Yes, but now is not the moment. Do go away, Perry. You can hardly hope to disguise your height, even beneath such a splendid cavalier costume! And if we are seen too much together, people will surely guess who I am."

The rose domino was soon in great demand. Even the Regent, coming late to the preceedings, had paused upon seeing her and vowed that he eagerly awaited the unmasking. She came face to face with Celestine, magnificent as Cleopatra, and was delighted to find herself unrecognized.

But she was less fortunate with Gervase. It was in the *chaîne Anglais* of a quadrille that he first encountered her—and frowned suddenly.

"Have you taken leave of your senses?" he murmured as they passed.

Her hand withdrew swiftly from the brief contact and with a husky "Pardon?" she moved on into the next sequence, but she knew the reprieve would be brief. And indeed, almost immediately afterward and against strong opposition, the rose domino found herself seized from behind and carried off into a waltz. She had no need to guess the identity of her captor. No one else, even shielded by the anonymity of the masquerade, would dare to hold her so close. Her heart, beating right up in her throat, prohibited speech and he seemed reluctant to spoil the moment.

But finally he said in a voice that sounded more clipped than usual, "I don't know whose crazy idea this was, but I presume you are aware of the possible consequences should anything go wrong?"

From the winged mask, her eyes glinted up at him in silence.

"Don't play off those tricks on me, my dear. You may have fooled everyone else in a quite masterly fashion, but they don't know that beautiful brooding mouth of yours half so well as I do!" He had the satisfaction of hearing her gasp and went on relentlessly. "I do trust that you mean to vanish before your coach turns back into a pumpkin?"

"Why should it matter to you?" she whispered in a choked voice.

"It doesn't," he replied with maddening complacence. "I was thinking of your beloved Signor Pucci who is like to find his pretty little piper ostracized by those outraged members of the *ton* who call the tune and who dislike above all to be made to look fools. And all for the sake of making a point!" Fury rose up in her; she tried to break free of him, but he only laughed softly. "You see how well I read your mind, even now!"

"Let me go!" she hissed, and found his arm tightening instead.

"Careful, *carissima mia*, your performance is slipping! And besides, the waltz is not yet at an end." He swirled her around in the most intimate way, contriving as he did so to brush her mouth with his. "At a

116

masquerade ball, you see, almost anything is allow-able!"

When the music ended, he led her off the floor with exaggerated politeness. He bowed. "May I procure a drink for you, ma'am?"

Without answering she almost ran from him.

"Who *is* that rose domino?" Celestine asked Gervase as she rushed past.

"Can't you guess?"

Celestine's mouth grew round and then broke into that wide, gamin grin. "But, of course! How droll!"

Meanwhile, Marissa found Perry and begged him to take her out into the garden.

"Are you all right, Marissa?" he eyed her anxiously. "Not got one of your headaches?"

"No, no, I'm fine!"

"You haven't been rumbled?" he urged.

"Rumbled?"

"Been recognized. You know!"

"Oh!" She hesitated then. "No," she said in a flat voice, "but I think I shall go home very soon."

"But there's *ages* left before you need do that! Oh, don't go, dearest!"

The endearment made her flinch. Out here in the garden there were colored lanterns everywhere strung out among the trees, making it seem almost as bright as day—the stillness disturbed now and then by fleeing figures and squeals of mock fear as some overly bold blade tried to anticipate the unmasking ceremonies. All the night scents of grass and honeysuckle, of roses and all kinds of nameless flowers were there, haunting Marissa with their sweetness, bringing back the memory of another night . . . *In such a night did young Lorenzo swear he loved her well, stealing her soul with many vows of faith, and ne'er a true one.* Who was it said that comparisons were odi-

117

ous? He was right. They simply made one feel much worse!

She cleared her throat. "Yes, but I am rather tired. And you need not miss the fun. If you will but see me to the carriage . . ."

A cry cut into what she was saying; no playful inducement, this, but a genuine plea for help. Just ahead of them in the shadow of a tree, a couple struggled, the girl protesting, the young man, also a cavalier, growing more insistent. Perry strode forward full of indignation, seized the young man by the shoulder of his splendid coat, and swung him around. The two cavaliers glared glitteringly at one another through their masks.

"Now, look here . . ."

"Off with you, sirrah!" commanded Perry from his superior height. "The young lady does not appear to favor your advances, so if you don't wish to have your cork drawn . . ." He left the alternative in the air and after a moment's hesitation the miscreant sloped off.

"Masterly, Perry!" cried Marissa who had already gone to the aid of the girl—a very young, very frightened shepherdess. "See, my dear child, there is a seat here in this little arbor where you may rest until you feel able to return indoors. The overardent young man has gone, so you can have nothing to fear."

But the girl, with surprising resilience, was already in a fair way to recovering her spirits, sufficiently so in any case to be showing a more than cursory interest in her rescuer.

"Perry?" she exclaimed, as though hardly daring to believe her eyes and ears. "Oh, Perry, is it really you?"

"By Jupiter!" Perry came quickly across the grass. "I say, can it be . . . Sal?" He peered closer. "It's never little Sally Morton!"

Shyly the girl removed her mask to reveal a face of

innocent sweetness rather than any great beauty, with eyes that, even by lantern light revealed quite clearly a marked degree of adoration for the young man standing before her.

"Lord! I'd no notion you were in Town, let alone at this affair tonight!" Perry was momentarily overcome. "But what is your mama about, letting you slope off into the garden with any loose fish that comes along?" He sounded quite severe and un-Perry-like. "It ain't at all the thing, y'know, Sal."

"No," she agreed meekly, and then, a little less so, "But you are doing it, are you not?"

"That's different. Oh, I say . . ." The embarrassing difficulty of having to introduce the girl he was to have married to the woman he loved assailed him suddenly; but Marissa had already guessed who she was and had quietly slipped away.

Chapter 9

"Gervase, have you seen Perry anywhere?" Lady Kitty grasped his arm with so much urgency that he was convinced she must have discovered the identity of the rose domino, but he would not commit himself to comment, saying merely, "No, my dear, but then, your brother's movements are of no particular interest to me."

"Well, he must be found—and quickly!" She lowered her voice. "You will never believe . . . the most dreadful thing has happened and I scarcely know what to do for the best. So embarrassing . . ."

By now convinced that she knew of Marissa's presence, he was about to offer some advice when the cowled figure of Sir Edward Kilroy joined them. Kitty turned to him eagerly.

"Edward—at last! Have you found him?"

"'Fraid not, m'dear," said her spouse, adding with what she could only consider to be a distinct lack of sensitivity. "Saw Lady Freemantle, though. Fact is, you could hardly fail to see her. I believe she is supposed to be Madame Pompadour, but I doubt old Louis would give her a second glance an' she were!"

"Dearest, I do wish you will be serious." Though the picture he conjured up caused her mouth momentarily to quiver, Kitty's voice was reproachful. It was a sad fact that though Edward adored her as much if not more than when they were first married, he no longer rushed like a knight to her rescue at the least whiff of disaster; though this surely constituted more than a mere whiff. "Oh, really, was there every anything more provoking!" she wailed. "That boy is never to hand when he is most needed!"

"I have no wish to appear inquisitive," murmured Gervase dryly. "But perhaps if I may be allowed to know why you want Perry so desperately . . . ?"

"You mean she hasn't told you?" Edward, in the act of taking snuff, offered his box to his friend with a laconic grin. "Lady Morton has arrived in Town, complete with offspring—she whose troth was to have been plighted to that young jackanapes, Perry—until he discovered more exotic waters to fish!"

"Edward! It is very well for you to make light of the whole thing, but you cannot have the least idea how I felt when I almost ran into Lady Morton just now! It seems that she and Sally are actually staying with Lady Chessborough! Thank heaven she did not immediately recognize me, but it only wins us a brief reprieve. If Perry is not warned, matters could turn exceedingly awkward!"

"More so than you realize, I fear." Gervase told them about the rose domino. Kitty let out a little shriek which caused several heads to turn. "Gently, my dear, we don't want to draw unwarranted attention this way . . ."

"True! Can't have any embarrassing incidents," the irrepressible Edward agreed. "Not with Prinny here! D'you know, I do believe he's wearing his corset tonight. Is it true, Ger, that he leaves it off altogether when he's down at Brighton?"

Kitty glared at him through the slits in her mask. "How can you even think about the Prince Regent at a time like this?"

"Your husband, my dear Kitty, is an unfeeling brute," said Gervase soothingly. "But do pray calm yourself. With a little judicious planning all may not yet be lost. Do see if you can find Perry and explain matters to him and I will engage to spirit Marissa out of harm's way."

But when he looked, she, too, had apparently vanished.

Marissa was not sure how long she had been walking in the gardens. The night was pleasantly warm and she had a great deal to sort out in her mind. Until now, she had truly believed that the girl back home for whom Perry was expected to offer had been a childhood playmate, no more—a match arranged by both parents in which neither had any say. But what she had seen in young Sally Morton's eyes when they rested on Perry had little to do with childhood friendships; and Sally's love and total trust in his ability to do what was right must foster in him, though he might not immediately be aware of it, a more mature, responsible attitude to life and love.

And now that she knew, there could be no question of what must happen next. Perry must be gently eased out of her life and encouraged to see in Sally Morton all those qualities which he supposed he had found in her. The slight ache in her throat was determinedly banished; it had been very pleasant to be put on a pedestal, just for a little while, but a pedestal could grow vastly uncomfortable in the end and she had always known that it was no more than an interlude.

Marissa retraced her steps once more until the lights of the house became visible. All desire to rejoin the festivities had left her, as had any thought of brazening out the unmasking ceremony. She doubted whether she would ever have gone through with that anyway. Gervase was right; it would hurt Cosmo and achieve nothing. However, she must call up Perry to render her one last service. If she had known how to find her way to the carriage without troubling him, she would have done so, but she was not perfectly sure where it awaited them.

She had almost reached the long, open windows when a figure in a black domino stepped from the shadows. There had been several among the revelers, but one in particular had appeared to follow her persistently. She had been obliged to dance with him at one point, but since he had been as silent as she, there had been little to identify him. It was ridiculous the way his silence had unnerved her. And now he was here yet again.

"Come," he said in a muffled voice and attempted to drag her away.

"Let me go this instant!" She was more angry than frightened as she strenuously resisted his efforts, and as though enraged by her unwillingness, he pulled her roughly into a crushing embrace that she was powerless to break, her cry cut off abruptly as his mouth came down on hers, cruelly bruising, probing, without any vestige of pleasure or kindness. Attempts to kick his shins with her soft slippers proved futile. There was something unutterably sinister about the total silence of his assault upon her, and she was in real dread of what might happen next when the sound of a footfall, a stone rattling on the path, made him lift his head. But her respite was only momentary as he said again, thickly, "Come!" and renewed his attempt to carry her off. His hand covered her mouth to stop her crying out and she bit it, hard. The man muttered an oath and, clutching at the injured member, blundered off into the darkness.

"My apologies," said Gervase with a calmness he was far from feeling. "But perhaps in the circumstances my arrival was to some degree . . . fortuitous?"

"Oh, yes! How glad I am that it is you!" Marissa

123

cried, throwing herself upon him in her relief and quite forgetting that they had parted but a short time ago, scarcely on speaking terms. "That man was attempting to . . . to . . ." She faltered.

"Yes, I rather thought he was! Perhaps, if you did not make yourself *quite* so irresistible?"

"I did not . . . I have not . . ." she began indignantly, but her voice caught on a sob and her teeth were beginning to chatter. With an exclamation he pulled her close, holding her with a kind of rough gentleness.

What a fool I am, she realized in a moment of blinding revelation, her face against his shoulder. What does anything else matter when this is where I belong? She lifted her head to tell him so when he put her from him, and taking her hand, said, a shade whimsically, "Now I mean to spirit you away, *cara mia*—I do hope you don't mean to bite me!"

At once she felt herself repulsed; an attempt to snatch her hand away failed. "There is no need to put yourself to the trouble. I shall find Perry . . ."

"Perry is not available at this moment," he said, unmoved. "And time, I fear, is pressing." They were already in the long gallery leading to the front door. "Did you have a cloak?"

"No, but . . ."

"Good. Then we can go at once."

Marissa disliked the feeling of being hustled away at his behest rather than her own. At that moment there was a cheer and a shout of "Tally-ho! Here she is, by Jupiter!" and a group of revelers came charging down the staircase. She shot a triumphant glance at Gervase and pulled herself free of his hand. Only as she moved forward and heard "Now we shall know—don't let her escape!" did she realize their purpose.

In a panic she was aware that Gervase was moving again to her side; also that the front door stood tantalizingly close, watched over by a footman who waited, stolidly oblivious of what was going on, ready to open it. Gervase shouted "No!" as she ran toward it and there were whoops of delight from her delighted pursuers. She evaded first one and then another until with blessed relief she heard Gervase again, his voice clear and calm: "Enough, my dear. We are vastly outnumbered, as you can perceive." And to the others, "Gentlemen! I pray you! You would not, I am persuaded, seek to usurp a privilege which must surely be due to your hostess!"

Their bubble pricked by the undoubted voice of authority, the young revelers good-naturedly surrendered their claim, though one aggrieved voice was heard to murmur that such initiative was deserving of *some* reward. But Gervase was unrelenting. He held out a hand which Marissa had little option but to take.

"I fear your anonymity cannot now be preserved. But if we can present you with true style, all might not yet be lost."

She had no idea what he intended, but was content to leave all to his judgment. She had ample time to reflect upon her own willful behavior as they mounted the staircase together, for if she was honest with herself, little blame could be attached to Perry over this evening's piece of work; she had come out of sheer pique—a determination to prove to Gervase that she could enter his world as an equal and carry it off. Was it not ironic that he must now rescue her from her own folly? Oh, she must have been mad! She was mad, knowing how fickle a thing was the popularity she enjoyed, with what disastrous ease it could be destroyed!

All too soon, it seemed, they had reached the head of the ballroom steps. There was a sudden hush; a sea of faces turned expectantly in rippling waves of brilliant light and color; the faint patter of spontaneous applause added an unsought touch of mockery to the proceedings.

Eyes glinting through the slits in his mask, Gervase offered Marissa his arm; she acted instinctively, responding in kind by laying her fingers upon it with the air of a queen bestowing a favor upon her knight.

"Splendid! Now, *carissima*, this will have to be the best performance you have ever given! Your deepest curtsy, if you please, when we arrive."

With figure proudly erect, she walked beside him down the length of the room, apparently oblivious of the crowd lining their path and closing in behind them, but very much aware of certain of the *grandes dames* whose rigid conventions she had flouted. She glimpsed Countess Lieven, Lady Jersey, and the exceedingly disagreeable Mrs. Drummond Burrell—all high-nosed patronesses of Almack's, the hallowed portals of which she would never be permitted to enter, though they had been gracious enough to her in their way. It was highly probable that this escapade of hers would bring down upon her their coldest disapproval—and where they led, how many more would follow?

At the far end of the room Lady Chessborough waited, the three curling plumes which adorned her coiffure lending added stature to an already imperious figure. In spite of, or perhaps because of the extreme delicacy of the moment, Marissa was obliged to stifle an irreverent desire to giggle; she looked so exactly like Madame Brunel at her most formidable. But the mammoth magnificence of the Prince Regent at her side exercised an instant sobering effect upon her. No doubt he had been lured from the card room by an overwhelming curiosity which—she swallowed nervously—was about to be gratified. She knew that her hope lay with him. His reaction would set the tone

126

for the rest—and though he might applaud her audacity in private, she could not know how he would respond with all eyes upon him.

Though she was the performer, it was Gervase who now held the stage, and this he did superbly well, exerting every ounce of his considerable charm; as she sank into a deep graceful obeisance, he doffed his mask, made an elegant leg to each in turn, and addressed himself to his hostess.

"My dear ma'am, I stand before you confessedly guilty of practicing a small deception which I trust you, in your boundless generosity, will pardon."

Lady Chessborough's proud features melted into something approaching coyness. Nothing Mr. Maxwell contrived, she assured him, could ever be other than in the best of taste and she had every confidence that it would be found to be so in this instance.

"You give me cause to hope, ma'am."

The Prince was jovially impatient. "Tell us now, Maxwell—this little deception of yours, may we deduce that it concerns this delightfully mysterious creature?" His fingers hovered tantalizingly close to Marissa's bent head. "If so, I vow you have us vastly intrigued!"

Gervase bowed, his smile tinged with irony. "Then our fate must rest upon the extent of Your Royal Highness's approval, for I confess that it was devised with just such an end in mind—a trifling jest contrived for your amusement which we now reveal to you."

Marissa knew that her moment had come. With every appearance of confidence she put back her hood, loosed the strings of the mask, and removing it, lifted her head slowly from its act of homage to give the Prince the mischievous smile which had in its depths that beguiling plea for understanding which had made her portrayal of Cherubino such a success.

127

There was a concerted gasp from those near enough to see which spread swiftly as a sibilant whispering to the back of the crowded room as the Prince Regent reached down with both hands to raise her up, his plump, raddled face creased into folds of unfeigned mirth.

"Well! Well now!" he said over and over while the frozen shock on Lady Chessborough's face hastily formed itself into the semblance of pleasurable surprise. "Nothing could be more handsome, what? A most agreeable idea, Maxwell!" The Prince all but nudged his hostess. "I doubt *you* knew of this all along, dear ma'am! How clever of you to sustain the secret so well! And now, my little signorina, you must pay the price for deceiving us—at least one song, I trust?"

Marissa, light-headed with relief, was only too happy to comply. Had His Royal Highness any preference, she asked.

He chuckled. "Oh, I think we must have our Cherubino, don't you?"

As she stood waiting to sing, Marissa's eyes scanned the crowd to see if she could pick out the black domino, but none stood out from the rest, and with little to distinguish her assailant, she was obliged to abandon the task and apply herself instead to winning back any temporary loss of face. That this was achieved more easily than she might have hoped for was due almost entirely to the Regent who by his very effusiveness made his feelings plain to all. The applause at the conclusion of her aria was therefore as enthusiastic as ever, and although she was obliged to endure much comment, some kind, some less so, no one actually shunned her.

She looked for Gervase, to thank him, but seeing him in conversation with Prinny and Countess

Lieven, held back. Whatever was said caused him to laugh and Madame de Lieven to tap his wrist reprovingly with her fan. Shortly afterward, much to her surprise, Madame de Lieven stopped to speak to her, a small smile playing about her lips.

"You dare much, Signorina Merrilli! But be advised by me and have a care lest one day Mr. Maxwell should not be at hand to rescue you from your indiscretions!"

Marissa swallowed her pride and dipped a curtsy in thanks. The Countess nodded graciously and passed on, with the air of one who knew that a word from her carried almost as much weight socially as did the more obvious approval of the Regent.

Celestine was upon her as soon as Madame was out of earshot, demanding to be told all. Marissa told her as much as seemed appropriate, making no mention of what had happened in the garden.

"But what slyness, *chérie!* To have had this in your mind for so long and not a word to me! I should scold you severely were the whole thing not so diverting! And is Gervase not the sly one? Not only does he rescue you in fine style, but somehow he persuades Madame de Lieven to notice you when one might have expected her total disapproval. I wonder, how *did* he induce her?"

"I have no idea," said Marissa a trifle impatiently. A moment ago she had been wishing to thank Gervase; now, with a perverseness she had not known she possessed, she resented the fact that everyone was applauding his part in the affair and was in a fair way to convincing herself that she might have done almost as well alone. In this frame of mind she greeted Perry with more warmth than she would otherwise have done as he pushed his way through the crush to shower her with apologies.

"If only you hadn't wandered off alone, dearest!" he

reproached her. "I know Gervase is a great gun and all that, but it was I who was responsible for you, after all. I looked everywhere! We both looked and then I thought that I had better take Sally back to the ballroom."

"I'm sorry," she said meekly. "I thought perhaps you would appreciate a few minutes with your friend."

"But it wasn't necessary to leave us alone. Sally and I have known one another forever!" He shuffled uncomfortably. "I daresay you will have guessed that it is she who . . . Sally is the one . . ."

"Your parents wish you to marry? Yes, I thought it might be so. She is very pretty."

"But terribly young and not half so beautiful as you! I fear there may be a little awkwardness—oh, not from Sally, you understand—she's wonderful, but her mother is here with her and, well, I'm not too sure how she'll take to the idea!" He seized her hand. "See—there is Kitty and Edward is with her. I have just time to make you known to him before the next sets begin to form."

As he had foretold, Marissa liked Sir Edward Kilroy from the very first. He was large and amiable, with reddish hair and eyes that crinkled at the corners when he smiled, as now.

"So you are the young lady who has been making young Perry look so moonfaced of late! Well, of course, now that I behold you the matter is fully explained. You are plainly a diamond of the first water!"

Kitty smiled in concurrence with her husband's remarks, but she scarcely heard what he said. She had endured a most trying evening and lived in dread of seeing Lady Morton approach. If only the dancing would begin and then presumably Perry would carry Signorina Merrilli away and a confrontation might be avoided for a little longer. She could not feel that her brother was half so troubled as he ought to be. He had actually admitted to her quite cheerfully that he had seen Sally, but without so much as a word about whether anything had been said to the poor child. Really, the whole affair was becoming dreadfully tiresome—and it was not even her place to deal with it. She wished very much that she might go home. Instead, she found the glorious embodiment of Madame Pompadour bearing down upon her in the person of Amabel Freemantle.

"Kitty, my dear! I felt sure it must be you. I remember that blue domino quite distinctly! You had it for the Scattergood's masquerade, did you not? And, if I am not mistaken, the Toutledge's little affair last year?"

"I am particularly fond of this domino!" said Kitty defiantly.

"But, of course, my love—and so you should be! Such a pretty color. It becomes you exceeding well!" She glanced around coyly. "Now, where is that bad boy, Perry? Ah, there you are! Surely you cannot be trying to hide from me?"

Perry, striving to be polite, stepped from Edward's shadow to give her a sickly smile which vanished as soon as it had come.

"It may surprise you to know, dear boy, that I penetrated your . . . signorina's disguise almost at once."

Kitty did not believe her for one moment—if Amabel had known the identity of the rose domino, it would have been all around the room within a matter of minutes; in a moment of indignation, she was so unwise as to tell her so. Lady Freemantle bristled visibly.

"I hope I know when to be discreet, my dear Kitty. I am persuaded that it is a trait only acquired when one has been about the world a little, so I do not presume to ring a peal over your brother with regard to his little social solecism which in charity one must attribute to youthful enthusiasm rather than any intended slight toward Lady Chessborough . . ."

Perry's face was red with the effort of keeping his indignation in check. "Perhaps you will be good enough to explain to me, ma'am, the nature of my indiscretion."

"Easy, m'boy!" Sir Edward, at his elbow counseled softly.

"Come now, Perry!" Lady Freemantle gave him an arch look from under plucked brows. "We have known one another for so long that I am persuaded I need not fear to be thought *interfering* if I speak my mind. Your partiality for the signorina is obvious to all who know you well and I am sure that you are not to be blamed for it, so charming as she is . . ." She nodded in a condescending way to Marissa whose color was also rising dangerously. "But, to be foisting one's"—she lowered her voice—"one's inamorata upon Lady Chessborough is the outside of enough! For, in spite of Mr. Maxwell's quite brilliant little charade just now, I find it inconceivable that he would ever be guilty of any such breach of good manners!"

The atmosphere was by now so charged with the force of emotions struggling for expression within the breasts of those concerned that the only question seemed to be who would explode first. As it happened, it was Kitty, sweet, mild Kitty, her nerves worn to a shred, for whom Amabel's final thrust had been one too many. The look of mingled rage, misery, and indignation upon Perry's face touched her to the core; she could even feel for Marissa whose distress was equally apparent, though she mistook its cause. What right had anyone to come between these two if they truly loved one another? She was suddenly very calm, speaking with a quiet dignity.

"You have a busy tongue, Amabel, which is never

happier than when it is making mischief." She ignored the gasp of outrage which greeted this home truth. "But this time you are sadly out. Signorina Merrilli and my brother are on the point of becoming betrothed. It would have been announced sooner but for poor Mama's indisposition." Her voice, though quiet, carried sufficiently well to attract some attention from those nearest to them.

"Kitty! Oh, my poor Kitty, what *have* you done?" murmured Edward ruefully, moving with unhurried gait to his wife's side.

Everyone else seemed to have been deprived of speech; even Lady Freemantle, for whom such a public dressing-down must have seemed like a nightmare, could only gape, blank-eyed. Perry too felt that he must be dreaming and Marissa could have wept. After one shocked glance she ceased to heed any of them; her glance was directed rather at a pretty little shepherdess standing no more than a few feet away who seemed suddenly to be all eyes in a paper-white face.

Marissa was hardly conscious of Lady Freemantle sweeping away in high dudgeon, or of anything going on around her until Perry took her hand, saying eagerly, "Well, I must say, though I'd liefer it hadn't happened in quite this way, Kitty's turned up a regular trump!" His smile grew gently teasing. "You can hardly refuse to name the day now, dearest Marissa!"

She looked around to find Lady Kitty just about bearing up with a little gentle encouragement from her husband.

Meeting Marissa's glance, Kitty managed a rather awkward smile. "Oh, dear, I do hope you are not angry?"

"No, indeed." Marissa infused some warmth into her voice, for after all, the damage was now done.

"But I should not have acted as I did! No one can

133

be more fully conscious of that fact than I! Quite apart from other consideration, it is not the ideal way to announce an engagement, except, of course"—her eyes sought Edward's for reassurance—"I couldn't possibly allow Amabel to get away with saying all those abominable things about Perry, could I?"

Edward agreed blandly that it was more than flesh and blood could be expected to support, and Perry said he didn't know why she should be making such a drama out of it all.

"I am vastly obliged to you, dear sister, for putting within my reach that which I desire above all else." He looked fondly at Marissa who tried to simulate some, at least, of his enthusiasm.

"Yes, that is very well, but only consider how awkwardly I have placed you! You will have to let Mama and Papa know at once, because a notice must now be sent to the *Gazette*, and if Papa should chance to read of your betrothal before he hears the news from you, he will be exceedingly angry . . . which I am very much afraid he will be, anyway. And *what* I am to say to Lady Morton, I dare not think! I suppose I couldn't fall victim to a sudden fainting fit?" Kitty looked hopefully at Edward who shook his head. She sighed. "You are right. I am not given to fainting spasms in the general way and someone would be sure to remark upon it and draw conclusions. Besides which, it would be very poor-spirited of me." The sigh deepened. "We must simply meet trouble as it comes. At least you two young things have got what you wanted."

It was perhaps fortunate that Lady Kitty was so preoccupied; but Edward was less so and Marissa encountered a faintly quizzical look from that deceptively genial, prosaic gentleman which brought a little color to her cheeks. She was relieved when Perry took her hand and carried her off presently to where the sets were forming for a cotillion.

Just for a moment she found herself next to Gervase and attempted to thank him for what he had done, and was met with a blistering shaft of cynicism which, after his earlier kindness, took her by surprise.

"My dear signorina, I begin to believe that you have but to pull the strings and we all dance to your bidding!" Her puzzlement brought a smile of pure mockery. "Such innocence! Such an actress! I kiss my hands to you! You wish to be accepted by the *ton*—and I make it possible. Now, I hear I am to felicitate you. How very fortunate—to have all your ambitions realized at a stroke!"

Chapter 10

It was impossible for Marissa to leave the ball early without causing further comment, so it was well into the early hours of the morning before she arrived home exhausted from the effort of showing a happy face to the world and to Perry in particular.

She had hoped to reach the haven of her room unobserved, but Tia Giannina, as zealous as a watchdog in her behalf, waited at the head of the stairs in a voluminous wrap, her voice a thunderous whisper.

"So? And how was your fine masquerade? You do not appear overjoyed as one would expect."

"I am tired. That is all."

Marissa walked past the signora into her room, threw the mask aside, and flopped down with a sigh onto the bed.

"Of course you are tired! Is it not well on the way to morning? Such hours to keep! And a Command Performance to be given later in this week! What is the Lord Marlowe about, to encourage such foolishness?"

"Tia Giannina, please! Could your inquisition not wait until morning?"

"Inquisition!" Signora Tortinallo's bosom heaved with indignation, but the demonstration went unnoticed; she peered closer, but Marissa would not meet her eyes. The voice softened imperceptibly. "Ah, well." A shrug. "Maybe you should get to your bed. But first, you will not neglect the Maestro."

Marissa lifted her head slowly. The hood of her domino fell back to reveal a pinched face and eyes shadowed by more than tiredness. "Oh, but . . . surely he will not have waited *so* long?"

"When does he ever rest—until you are safely home?"

It was true. But it was with dragging step that she made her way to Cosmo's room. He could read her even better than Tia Giannina and in her present mood it was beyond her capabilities to deceive him. But Luigi, the signor's valet, met her at the door and informed her with shades of reproof imperfectly concealed that his master had succumbed out of sheer weariness and was even now sound asleep.

His pronouncement should have cheered Marissa, but rather she felt only an overwhelming sense of rejection. Never before had he done such a thing. Her throat filled and tears of self-pity pricked her eyes. She slept badly and snapped at Maria when she brought her chocolate late in the morning; upon spilling some on the coverlet she was scolded by Tia Giannina. It did not auger well for the day ahead.

Cosmo would have to be told. She did not relish the task, but as with most disagreeable tasks she preferred to get it over quickly. The moment she entered the drawing room, however, some instinct told her that she had been spared the necessity. He was seated in his usual chair beside the fireplace with his small portable desk before him and the score of the new opera laid out on a sofa table at his elbow.

He looked up as she entered and such was the rapport between them that she knew his mood at once. Girding herself to brave his displeasure, she came to take up her favorite position at his feet, one arm resting against his knee. When he did not speak she tried a little gentle raillery.

"You are angry with me, I think?"

The glance that met hers was distant, unsmiling. "Not angry, precisely. Shall we say, rather, disappointed."

Marissa's heart turned over. "But why? Do I not have a right to know?"

"By a curious chance you voice my own sentiments, almost exactly." Signor Pucci's lips twisted wryly. "Maybe advancing senility induces a certain degree of childishness, for I find that I care quite violently that news of your betrothal to Lord Marlowe should need to be imparted to me from an outside source." He inclined his head. "I realize, of course, that you are of age and owe me little perhaps other than loyalty ..."

"I owe you everything!" Marissa cried passionately. "I would not have you hurt for the world! What I do not understand is how you came to learn of something which happened quite spontaneously in the early hours of this morning?"

"So you do not deny the engagement?"

"That it happened? No! But that it was in any way preconceived—" Marissa thrust angry fingers into her hair, tumbling it into heedless disarray. "Yes, that I do most vigorously disavow! How could you believe that I would contemplate such a step without first confiding it to you?"

Signor Pucci extended a frail graceful hand to prop up her chin and her beautiful jade eyes stared back at him, glistening with angry unshed tears.

"I am rebuked," he said dryly, so that she gave a funny hiccuping laugh and brushed a hand impatiently across her eyes. "Very well. If you wish to confide in me now, I will listen."

"You won't like it very much," she told him frankly, but the story poured out, nonetheless.

He heard her out in silence, then spoke quietly. "You should not have gone, but for that I must bear some of the blame. I fear I did not perfectly comprehend what you intended until Severin came to see me last evening on his way to the very same ball." So absorbed in his story was he that he did not notice Marissa's sudden frown. "Sir Hugo seemed . . . surprised to know that you had been invited. Only then did I fully understand. He was so good as to promise that he would see you came to no harm as a result of your impetuosity, but it appears that Mr. Maxwell was the quicker to act. I am obliged to him."

Marissa said, "If Sir Hugo was at the ball I did not see him. Was he in costume?"

"No." Signor Pucci thought for a moment. "I believe he carried a black domino over his arm."

The black domino! So it was Sir Hugo! Marissa remembered how he had behaved, and a tide of embarrassment swept the color into her face.

"Is something amiss, child?"

"No . . ."

Signor Pucci regarded the bent head with some concern, wishing that it was within his power to extricate her from the situation in which she found herself; always supposing that she needed his help. He touched the tumbled hair lightly.

"Forgive me, *cara*, but I must ask you—are you content to marry Lord Marlowe?"

Content! "No," she admitted without raising her head. "It was the very last thing I wished to happen! And somehow I must find a way to undo what has been done."

"So you are not in love with him?" He managed to keep the relief from his voice.

"No! Oh, Perry is a charming boy and I am conscious that I have made shameful use of him in the past, but . . ."

"But he is a boy, nonetheless," Signor Pucci finished for her. "And you are in love with someone else, perhaps?"

139

Her head came up slowly, the jade-green eyes widely questioning, faint telltale color staining her cheeks.

He smiled reassuringly. "You cannot hide such things from me, *cara mia*. My whole life has been devoted to the study of the human voice—a most delicate instrument, it is tuned irrevocably to the pitch of our emotions and in consequence it reflects with absolute truth the forces of passion within us. Happiness and pain—a love affair—a little heartbreak—such agencies refine and mold the timbre of the voice until it becomes a true and exquisite expression of beauty!"

His words were so much an evocation of how she felt that it seemed for a moment as if her soul had been laid bare. The color in her cheeks deepened, though she could not confirm or deny his appraisal. But it seemed he did not expect any answer.

"I would not have presumed to speak of it in the ordinary way, but since the object of your affection is not Lord Marlowe ..."

He must not know about Mr. Maxwell—not just now, in any case. Not until she could talk about him rationally. She clambered hastily to her feet, panic evident in the very inelegance of the move, and turned away to stare deliberately out of the window. He was correspondingly curious.

He said casually, "I believe Sir Hugo would need very little encouragement to declare his regard for you, should you succeed in releasing yourself from this present entanglement ..." He watched for her reaction, but beyond a slight tightening of the shoulders, he could divine little. "It would be a match with many advantages, *cara*. Sir Hugo's interest in your career is clearly apparent, and it would please me to see you settled ..."

Marissa could not let him go on. "Please!" she implored him. "Could we not talk about it just now?"

She drew a quick breath, and turned with her feelings well in hand. "I can think of nothing until I am free to do so."

Tia Giannina chose that moment to enter the room, followed by a footman staggering slightly as he maneuvered through the door a most enormous basket of flowers which bore a card from her "adoring Perry." With her announcement that the first visitor was even now being admitted at the door, all further discussion was curtailed, the papers were hastily gathered up, and the ritual began. There were more callers than usual, drawn irresistibly by the events of the previous evening. Perry was very much in evidence, making up for any lack of effusiveness on Marissa's part by his own exuberance. Later, when most of the guests were on the point of leaving, Sir Edward and Lady Kilroy arrived to set the seal of approval upon the young couple—and dispel any hint of unharmoniousness within the family.

Kitty endeavored to draw Marissa to one side. "Can we talk?" she pleaded.

Marissa looked around. They would not be missed for a few moments. "Come," she said and led the way to an adjoining parlor where the sun poured in. She closed the door and turned to face Perry's sister.

Kitty was fidgeting with her gloves and was slow to begin. "I have hardly closed my eyes all night," she confessed at last, meeting Marissa's questioning glance; and as though to justify the remark added resolutely, "Well, I daresay it will not come as any surprise to you to know that I never wished for a union between you and Perry. In fact, until recently I have been quite actively opposed to any such union . . ."

"You asked Mr. Maxwell to separate us, did you not?" Marissa asked.

Kitty's blue eyes widened. "Why, however did you

. . . ? Well, it is no matter now for everything is changed!" She did not wish to be reminded of Gervase who had been almost short with her at the ball last night—and after he had positively encouraged her to recognize the signorina! "I have quite made up my mind that I shall stand by you and Perry, no matter what Mama and Papa may say," she continued quickly. "You and I must get to know one another much better, so I would like you to come to tea quietly with me as soon as possible—tomorrow afternoon, perhaps? And I mean to hold a small assembly before the Season ends, in order to present you properly to all our friends."

Marissa would have been better convinced, had she not rushed the words out rather as though she were swallowing a draught of horrid medicine. In spite of her deep depression of spirits, a glint of humor lurked in Marissa's eyes as she said with a sudden rush of candor, "You are very kind, but I would much liefer you helped me to find a way to relinquish my hold on Perry without hurt to him, which it was my intention to do before your somewhat . . . precipitate announcement."

Kitty's reaction was comical; astonishment, resentment on her brother's behalf at this seeming rejection, followed almost at once by consternation as she realized what she had done.

"You mean . . . you do not wish? You have no desire to . . . oh, what *have* I done? Goodness!" Finally as a sudden sense of the ridiculous came to her aid she dissolved into a peal of laughter, removed her bonnet to release her bright gold curls, and sank onto the sofa, patting the place beside her. "What a coil! Do come and sit down, *dear* Marissa—you do not mind if I call you Marissa?—and we will see what we can devise!"

By the time Marissa set out to drive in the Park

with Perry that same afternoon she was already feeling considerably more cheerful. The talk with Kitty had not only served to clear her head, it had also cleared the air between them and sown the seeds of a new friendship; for Kitty, having discovered somewhat tardily that Marissa posed no permanent threat to Perry, was very much more at her ease, and they had no sooner put their heads together over tentative plans for terminating the engagement than they were on the way to liking one another rather well.

"Are you quite sure that you do not wish to marry Perry?" Kitty asked, half jokingly. "I begin to think that I might quite enjoy having you for a sister."

Marissa returned a mischievous grin. "I would be sorely tempted had I not met my rival. Perry, you see, is infatuated with an ideal that doesn't exist. Sally Morton will suit him very much better, did he but know it. She looks up to him, you see, and that must bring out those most endearing qualities in him which prompt him to cherish and protect one as if one were a fragile flower. To be treated thus is very flattering, of course, the more especially when one is perfectly capable of fending for oneself!" She gave a self-denigrating shrug. "But marriage! Only consider Perry's disillusion upon discovering that his ideal has feet of clay when it is too late to mend matters! Better by far that he should know of my shortcomings now, don't you think?"

"I'm not sure what it is you are suggesting, but if I understand you aright, then I should say that you are behaving with great generosity," said Kitty slowly. "It is very difficult to believe that you are very little older than Perry."

"In actual years, no—but in the theater, you know, one grows up very quickly." Marissa smiled. "And besides, a pedestal can be a very uncomfortable place to remain for any length of time!"

They both agreed that nothing was to be gained by acting in haste. The engagement was a *fait accompli;* thanks to Kitty's impulsive announcement and Perry's eagerness to act upon it by notifying the *Gazette* and writing to his parents, to deny it now would raise more problems than it would solve, leaving Perry's pride in shreds.

"The great majority of people will be leaving Town very shortly," said Kitty comfortably, "and if we cannot, between us, contrive to steer Perry into Sally's arms before the start of next Season, then we do not deserve to succeed!" She sighed. "Our greatest obstacle will, I fear, be Papa!"

What Kitty had not reckoned upon was the extent of Lady Morton's grievance. A deep sense of affront filled her ladyship's breast and the quickest way to assuage it was to secure for her daughter a match that would cast young Lord Marlowe's former pretensions quite into the shade and demonstrate to her friends, in whom she had confided her expectations in that direction, that it had been no more than a childhood attachment upon both sides, and that, in effect, a gentleman who chose to attach himself formally to a "person of the theater" clearly revealed himself to be unworthy of a "Morton of Undershaw."

Her ladyship had set herself no easy task, however, the most eligible gentlemen having been snapped up earlier in the Season with the exception of those who, like Mr. Maxwell, must be accounted unattainable. But Lady Morton did not despair. Mrs. Drummond-Burrell had promised to send her vouchers for Almack's and had confided to her that the Marquis of Cheam was hanging out for a wife, his late spouse having departed this life after failing to provide him with an heir. Furthermore, it was rumored that Lord Cheam's pockets were badly to let owing to a strong partiality for games of chance.

Sally, with the promise of a generous dowry, plus a sizable inheritance from her late grandmother, and whose youthful prettiness and biddable disposition must count in her favor, might very well take his lordship's eye.

It never once occurred to Lady Morton that her daughter might not care to be married to a man old enough to be her father and possessed of a dubious reputation where women were concerned; she had been brought up to believe that a daughter obeyed her parents in all things, not least when it came to the choice of her husband.

The afternoon being fine and warm, the Park was busier than usual, with fluttering muslin skirts and brightly twirling parasols making a colorful display beneath the trees. The huge painted wheels of Perry's curricle lent a vivid splash of yellow to the scene, and drew many an admiring glance which extended to his companion who, in a paler shade of yellow, graced this splendid new equipage, a lacy white parasol shading her eyes from the sun.

They were obliged to stop quite often to receive congratulations from friends and well-wishers, though not everyone paid them this courtesy. But Perry was far too occupied in voicing enthusiastic plans for their forthcoming nuptials to notice when Lady Jersey smiled a cold little smile and passed on; nor was he aware that he did not have his love's whole attention, as, from time to time, she scanned the crowds hoping for a sight of that unmistakable, distinguished figure so seldom absent from the daily promenade. Each time sunlight caught the flash of silver beneath a high-crowned hat her heart leaped, only to plummet almost at once in disappointment. She saw Sir Hugo astride a raking bay horse. He inclined his head and thereafter stared at her in a strange intense fashion that made her feel uncomfortable, but made no attempt to approach, as they passed. She hoped, for Cosmo's sake, that he was not minded to turn against her and withdraw his patronage, though for her own part, after his extraordinary behavior of last night, she had rather forego the opera than be obliged to endure his closer attentions; from that much at least, her engagement to Perry must shield her for the present.

She put him resolutely from her mind as Perry commanded her attention, desirous to know whether she had any preferences regarding their honeymoon—a tour of the Continent, perhaps. Remembering her resolve to disillusion him by degrees, she replied airily that it was all one to her and reminded him that they could not in any case please themselves as she had definite commitments to fulfill. This made him a trifle sulky and at that precise moment she saw Sally approaching in a barouche with a lady whom she supposed to be Lady Morton. Marissa seized the opportunity to say casually, "Is that not your little friend from the country?"

The barouche drew almost level with them and, as Perry prepared to stop, went by them without any slowing of its pace, Lady Morton looking straight ahead as if they had not been there and Sally, with the smile of recognition wiped from her face, turning wistfully to look over her shoulder until she was sharply reprimanded and adjured in a carrying voice not to make herself look cheap.

Perry was full of angry indignation which found voice in the shaky assertion that he had never really *liked* Lady Morton, but she had always been civil with him until now.

"And I'm bound to say that I think it the shabbiest trick to serve on Sally! Did you see her face? Poor child, she looked quite stricken!"

Privately Marissa agreed with him; it was not a

pleasant experience to be cut in public as she had cause to know. But it was no part of her present plan to be sympathetic.

She said with ruthless logic, "Quite so, but it is no use your being dog in the manger about it, you know. I daresay Lady Morton has her daughter's best interests at heart. Since you have declined to suit for Sally's hand, I daresay she will wish to look about her for some alternative suitor—and the longer the child is encouraged to moon after you, the less she will wish to consider anyone else!"

Perry so far forgot himself as to jerk on the ribbons, causing his fine new pair of bay geldings to job at the bit. It took him several moments to bring them under control, by which time he was able to say with only a slight stiffness of manner that even Lady Morton would not stoop to rush so young a girl to the altar, and that he had not thought to hear her sounding so heartless.

Marissa moved her parasol forward a little to hide her face. So he was not indifferent to Sally's fate! She said demurely, "I am sorry if that is what you think. I was simply trying to see things from their viewpoint. Sally seems a charming girl. Surely it is not heartless in me to wish to see her as happily settled as we are?" She gave his arm a litle squeeze for good measure.

He did not respond with his usual eagerness and after a moment asked in rather too casual a way, "You don't suppose Sally really does cherish a definite tendre for me, do you?"

"Of course she does! I marked it most particularly in her eyes last evening in the garden—a woman notices these things, you know, much quicker than a man. But you need not fear that I am jealous, for I daresay it is no more than a girlish infatuation which will not last beyond her first few weeks in London. She is quite pretty in a *jeune fille* style and with any luck someone will soon come along to sweep her off her feet!"

Perry's reply was indistinct and Marissa, well pleased with her morning's work, did not pursue the matter further. For the rest of the drive he remained preoccupied, being much disturbed to find that he could not banish from his mind the memory of Sally's wistful face as she had looked back at them earlier; it recalled with almost painful clarity the moment during the ball when he had sought Sally out after she had been obliged to hear the news of his engagement in the worst possible way.

"Of course I understand, Perry," she had assured him with astonishing dignity and composure in one so young. "Your Marissa is *very* beautiful! I am not in the least surprised that you wish to m-marry her. I hope you will be very happy!"

It hadn't made him feel happy at the time and now, remembering, he admitted what he had not wanted to recognize at the time—that there had been a hurt in her eyes which she had not quite been able to hide.

Chapter 11

The Royal Command Performance exceeded all Marissa's expectations, surpassing even her Benefit night. It had been thought that, coming late in the Season, many of the fashionable might already have left Town, but if this were so, their absence was not felt. By the time the last of the carriages thronging the Haymarket had set down its precious burden before the gracious portals of the Opera House, the auditorium was full of bustle and brilliance, and glittered from pit to gallery as all awaited the arrival of the Prince Regent.

Mr. Maxwell's box occupied a prime position close to that of the Prince Regent and almost opposite the Kilroy's where Sir Edward and Lady Kitty were entertaining the Misses Phipps. Committed by Perdita Wellam to making up a party for the evening, he had sought to render it as agreeable as possible by including among his guests not only Celestine and Rupert, but also Mrs. Arbuthnot and her friend, the indolent Lady Drusilla, who so amused him with her odd ways.

As they waited, Gervase was the punctilious host, yet it was clear to those who knew him best that a part of his mind was elsewhere. Beside him, Perdita fluttered like a gaudy, restless butterfly, her empty prattle a faint irritant upon his senses. Something would have to be done about Perdita—and soon, he promised himself.

He had not seen Marissa since the night of Lady Chessborough's ball. This was a deliberate decision, for the quite irrational degree of anger he had felt upon hearing of her engagement to Perry that night had thrown him into a state of confusion—a novel and not very agreeable experience, only partially alleviated by Edward's wry disclosure of the circumstances. That their marriage had now become a very real possibility had so shaken him as to deprive him utterly of his night's sleep—a circumstance so unusual that Dobson had been cast into high fidgets upon finding his master sitting by the open window at five o'clock in the morning, it being as plain as plain that the bed had not been slept in.

Gervase had done a lot of thinking during those wakeful hours. He thought of Marissa married to Perry—married to anyone—and found the idea totally unacceptable. But why? Was it injured pride because she had rejected him—a pressing need to prove to her that he always got what he wanted in the end? Surely he was not *so* petty?

The sky paled to pearl and then grew faintly pink, the color deepening like the first blushes on a maiden's cheek as the sun prepared to lift its face to the new day; and with its first rays came the revelation that for perhaps the first time in his life he was not wholly able to command his emotions. Not one of the many beautiful women who had graced his life until now had ever roused in him the least desire to protect her from harm; still less had he ever contemplated a permanent relationship with even the most amusing of them. But with Marissa he no longer had a choice; he knew without a doubt that he wished nothing more than to spend the rest of his life with her—and if that meant marriage, then marriage it must be. So certain was he, that he saw Perry as nothing more than a trifling obstacle in his path.

Yet all his instincts urged caution; the fear of being rejected a second time, though unfamiliar to him, was nonetheless real and oddly humbling. The knowledge imparted to him in confidence by Kitty, that Marissa had no thought of going through with the marriage, relieved him in part of that fear, enabling him the better to school himself to patience for a time and await events ...

A general rustling, a craning of necks disturbed his thoughts and Gervase rose with the rest of the audience to greet the Prince Regent who had entered his box, beaming and nodding benevolently in response to the ovation. His brother, York, headed the impressive entourage that accompanied him.

Behind the stage, temperament was running high; the wait seemed interminable. Dancers in their bright flimsy gauzes practiced last-minute steps and got in the way of the other performers who snapped at them. Marissa was several times obliged to reassure Madame Brunel that she had no intention of usurping her position in the company and that it was of little account that the Prince had singled her out for attention.

"What does it matter?" she whispered in response to Tia Giannina's snort of disgust. "To Madame it is everything to be of first importance, and I have no wish to rob her of that accolade!"

The orchestra completed its tuning up and fell silent—and into the expectant hush that followed came the sound of cheering. The artistes took up their positions, and as the magnificent red-and-gold curtain was drawn slowly up, "God Save the King" was sung and the Regent, his party, and a great number of the audience joined enthusiastically in the chorus.

It was a memorable performance, one that was to be spoken of often in the future; the whole company gave of their best, but all agreed ungrudgingly in the end that Marissa was outstanding. She bubbled with vitality, her voice, never better, rang pure and clear, and when near the end of the evening she sang the aria "Care Selve" from Handel's *Atalanta*, many of her fellow performers as well as a large proportion of the audience were reduced to weeping, including Prinny who was quite visibly moved.

In the adjoining box Gervase could see Cosmo Pucci, the tears running down his face as he sat with Perry. When the curtain at last descended, he seemed dazed and loath to move. And then Gervase's attention was claimed by Celestine whose triumphant pleasure in Marissa's success was shared by all as they collected up their wraps and prepared to leave. They were on the point of doing so when the door to the box burst open and Perry rushed in.

"Gervase! Thank God you are still here! It's Signor Pucci . . . I don't know what to do!"

Gervase needed no bidding. He covered the ground between the two boxes so swiftly that Perry was almost obliged to run in order to keep up with him.

"It was awful, Ger! He was a little unsteady as he rose from his seat and I went to help him when he just sort of crumpled—without a sound!"

Kneeling by the unconscious man, Gervase loosened his cravat and felt for his pulse; it was there, shallow and uneven, his face was ashen, his skin clammy. "Perry, give me his cloak, quickly! Do you have one?" And as Perry shook his head, "Dammit, neither do I! Well, go next door. See what you can find." He was stripping off his coat as he spoke, folding it and placing it under Signor Pucci's head. "And, Perry—don't let anyone else in here for the present."

It was, however, Mrs. Arbuthnot who brought in her own cloak. "I'll not get in your way," she said brusquely, bending to sum up the signor's condition at a glance. "Bad, is he?"

"About as bad as he can be," said Gervase quietly without looking up. "I think perhaps Perry should fetch Marissa and Signora Tortinallo—they may know better what to do for him. But tell him, for God's sake, not to put them in a panic!"

There was a knock on the door and one of the Prince's aides put his head around. Word had reached His Royal Highness, he said. The Prince was most upset to learn that Signorina Merrilli's mentor had been taken ill and had offered to put his own retiring room entirely at their disposal.

"There is a comfortable couch," said the aide, "and a much greater degree of privacy would be afforded."

"His Royal Highness is very kind," Gervase regarded the frail figure pensively and lifted his eyes to meet Mrs. Arbuthnot's.

"It can't hurt, surely," she said, reading his mind. "If the signor is moved with care."

"Perhaps not. He can't stay here indefinitely, anyway."

The aide stepped forward to assist, but Gervase had already gathered the older man up in his arms. And this was how Marissa found them as she pushed her way breathlessly through the crowds, with Perry clearing her path and Signora Tortinallo some little way behind; Cosmo looking like a child in Gervase's arms, his face showing little more color than the frilled lace cuffs falling back frivolously from the hands that cradled him with such gentleness. She cried out and clutched at a fold of the spotless lawn sleeve.

"It's all right!" Gervase hushed her as he laid Signor Pucci down carefully, tucking the cloaks around him. The ashen face as yet showed no signs of returning consciousness, but his pulse seemed a fraction stronger. He told Marissa so, and his voice, quietly reassuring, seemed to calm her. She drew a steadying breath and stood away from him. Her eyes, still painted and ringed with black, looked huge.

"Forgive me," she said. "It was the shock . . ."

She suddenly became aware of the Prince who stood just inside the door conferring with his aides. Belatedly, she curtsied to him.

"No, no, dear young lady! We don't stand upon ceremony at a time like this!" he assured her, raising her up. His plump hands enfolded hers, patting them constantly in a sympathetic way. "Such a sad ending to a magnificent evening, what? But there, you won't care to talk of that just now. I doubt you will be wishing us at the devil, eh? Well, we don't mean to get in your way. But young Graily, here, shall remain," he wheezed, indicating the gentleman who had assisted Gervase. "Keep out any unwanted callers, don't y'know. Anything you want, m'dear, you just ask Graily—anything at all, mind!"

The Prince Regent was on the point of leaving when Signora Tortinallo erupted into the room, her fierce glance taking no account of mere princes as she sought out her beloved Maestro. She surged past, crossed to the couch, and bent over it, her voice scolding softly in Italian as she chafed the still, cold hands.

Marissa turned to make apologies on her behalf to the Prince, but he would not hear them and seemed amused as he took his leave and departed with his small retinue following in his wake.

A moment later the door opened again to admit Rupert and a tall gentleman with grisled hair and a genial countenance, who announced without preamble that he was Sir James Maclauchlin, a physician down from Edinburgh to visit a colleague.

Introductions were effected all around. "You have need of a doctor, I believe?" He smiled at Marissa. "That was a rare treat you gave us tonight, lassie—

quite brilliant!" His glance moved to Mr. Maxwell who appeared to be in charge of things and thereafter to the figure on the couch. "May I?"

"Surely." Gervase explained briefly what had happened.

Signora Tortinallo regarded the stranger balefully and gave place to him with obvious reluctance and only after Marissa had entreated her. She watched with deep suspicion every move of Sir James's examination.

"The gentleman has had this condition for some time?"

"Yes." Marissa felt a terrible guilt when she remembered how little Cosmo had regarded the cost to his own health in his obsession with her career. "Is he going to die?" she asked abruptly.

"My dear lassie, you are asking me an impossible question! It would be foolish in the extreme for me to venture a definite opinion at this stage." His eyes were indescribably gentle. "I can only say that I will do all in my power to bring him through; the rest is in the hands of God." He became brisk once more. "Firstly, we must get the wee man home to his own bed—and then we'll see."

He gave her an encouraging little nod and turned away to consult with Gervase upon the best way to transport Signor Pucci. Several ideas were considered; Perry suggested that a board might be found backstage upon which to lay him, but in the end it was decided that Gervase would carry him; that way he would best be shielded from the jolting of the carriage.

As she listened to them the hard cold knot inside Marissa's chest eased a little. Gervase, one could always trust, and Sir James—she could not decide just why he gave her such hope. Perhaps it was simply that he was such a large comfortable man—also, it was very hard not to be encouraged by a man who called one "lassie."

Mrs. Arbuthnot had waited only to see the signor safely bestowed before helping Gervase into his coat and returning to reassure the ladies of their party. And Rupert, having done all he could, engaged to see them safely home. Outside the door he found Sir Hugo enjoined in a hot altercation with the redoubtable Mr. Graily, who was steadfastly refusing to admit him.

"Go home, Severin," Rupert advised him without preamble. "There ain't a thing you can do in there, save get in the way. Not the time or place for a social call, d'you see?"

"Damn your insolence, Egerton!" Sir Hugo ground out, white-mouthed with cold rage. "I have more right in there than you. Signor Pucci and I . . ."

"Signor Pucci ain't receiving, I tell you. If you must know, he's unconscious and likely to remain so for some time. And if he ever does open his eyes again, which I take leave to doubt from the look of him, he'll not be wanting the likes of you jawing away at him. What's more," Rupert added with a pugnacious thrust of a chin and a quick sidelong glance at the Prince's man, "Marissa has enough to worry about at present without having to be pleasant to callers, so if you don't leave now, peaceably, young Graily here and I will be obliged to give you a helping hand!"

Mr. Graily, who had been listening in some awe to Rupert's outburst, endeavored to look suitably threatening.

Sir Hugo's eyes narrowed to angry slits. "Very well. I have no wish to institute an ugly brawl. But you had best have a care, Egerton. I don't take kindly to being ordered off, especially by a mere hanger-on like you!"

He walked swiftly away and Rupert and Mr. Graily exchanged wry glances.

Signor Pucci's journey home was achieved with the minimum of fuss, and he was soon being undressed and put to bed by a highly emotional Luigi, helped by Gervase. Sir James watched his patient carefully throughout as did Signora Tortinallo who had adamantly refused to leave even for a moment.

"Do you think I have not been through all of this before?" she demanded. "Mother of the Skies, who has a better right to tend the Maestro than I who have known him intimately these forty years and more!" If there was an added brightness in those fierce eyes she would have scorned to know it as they observed with vigilance each movement. And as if aggravated beyond endurance: "Luigi! If you are not able to do what is required of you without sniffling all over your master, you had better leave him to those who can!"

This naturally incensed the valet; he had not been spoken to in that way for many years. He became very excited and it was perhaps fortunate that his task was all but accomplished. Sir James admonished them both in a voice which brooked no argument, saying that his patient must have complete quiet and anyone unable to control their feelings could not be permitted to remain. He then made a further examination, grunted and expressed himself reasonably well satisfied. "With your permission I'll be away to fetch my bag and to urge my friends not to wait up for me. I should be back here within the hour." He looked across at Gervase. "I do not anticipate any crisis, but—you will be staying?"

Gervase nodded.

"Good, good." With consummate tact he addressed himself to the signora. "If the wee man should waken, you will oblige me by letting him move as little as possible. Rest is everything!" He gave her a reassuring smile. "Together we'll maybe pull him through this, yet."

Marissa, banned from the sickroom while Cosmo was put to bed, wandered disconsolately to her own room where Maria helped her out of her beautiful stage costume and into the flounced negligee. In a silence bristling with morbid curiosity she brushed out Marissa's hair and threaded a ribbon through it. Finally, as Marissa stood up to leave, came the agonized whisper.

"The Maestro, signorina—will he die?"

"No, of course not!" The curtness of the answer brought ready tears to the young maid's eyes. Marissa, seeing them, put out a quick consoling hand and said with gentle certainty, "No, I am sure he will not."

She had not heard the doctor leave so she made her way to the drawing room to await news. When the door opened she was standing aimlessly by Cosmo's chair, smoothing its back with restless fingers. She swung round as Gervase came in, her eyes mirroring piteously the question she could not voice. He told her exactly what the doctor had said, no more, no less.

"But it must be a good sign that he has left him, if only for a little while, don't you think?" she pleaded.

He agreed. There was a moment when they stood just looking at one another, Gervase, distressed by her pallor, but thinking nevertheless how enchanting she looked *en déshabillé.* Then he opened his arms and she walked into them without a moment's hesitation, as naturally as if she belonged there, which, as she was enfolded and her head came to rest against his shoulder, she realized that she did.

"Oh, I have been such a fool!" she confessed to his splendid brocade waistcoat.

"And I was too arrogantly sure of myself!" There was the merest ghost of a laugh in his voice. He smoothed her hair, lifted a strand, and allowed it to fall back. "It *is* like silk. You can't imagine how often I have been longing to do this!" He threaded gentle fingers into the dark rippling cloud and cupped her head between his hands, lifting her face to impart a kiss of infinite tenderness. For an instant she clung; then he sensed a reluctant withdrawal.

"We should not!" she pleaded. "There is Perry . . ."

"Ah, yes, of course. Perry!" He made no attempt to coerce her, holding her loosely in the circle of his arms; but though his mouth quirked wryly, his eyes grew suddenly intense. "He will have to be told, you know," he said with unaccustomed fierceness. "That you are mine!"

A faint color relieved Marissa's pallor. She leaned away a little to look up at him. "Am I? Truly?"

He kissed her again, more thoroughly this time. "Can you doubt it?" he said, lifting his head at last.

She fended him off with one hand, half laughing. "No. No more doubts. But, please, you will have to be a little patient. I *will* tell Perry, but in my own way . . . at the moment I cannot think quite straight . . ."

"And I, selfish brute that I am, should know better than to tease you with it now."

"Oh, no!"

He laughed softly and released her, but for that outflung hand which he captured and carried to his lips. "Very well. We will pretend a little longer. But I give you fair warning that though I am a patient man in most things, now that my heart is truly engaged, I shall be counting the hours!"

159

Chapter 12

The days that followed were anxious ones for Marissa
as Cosmo, after giving them all the most dreadful
fright, began the slow, painful fight for life. Sir
James was splendid, dispensing hope like a man pay-
ing out a lifeline in a rough sea, leaving one just
enough to keep one buoyant without ever becoming
overconfident. Marissa felt guilty lest they were en-
croaching too selfishly upon his time, but when she
confided as much to him, his eyes twinkled.

"Och, lassie, you've no call to worry on that score.
My time is my own, after all, and a doctor, like a
priest, is never quite free of his calling. Besides"—the
twinkle broadened into a chuckle—"'tis a poor man
who would deny himself the opportunity of seeing
your bonnie face every day!"

It was fortunate that the season at the Opera House
was coming to a close, for Tia Giannina was obviously being pulled two ways. Marissa, seeing this and
knowing that she would not be easy away from her
beloved Maestro for any length of time, asserted that
she could manage well enough with Maria for the
few remaining performances. And so Maria was pro-
moted to the dizzy heights of temporary dresser and,
in the opinion of the remaining servants, grew un-
bearably smug.

On the day following Signor Pucci's collapse the
knocker was never still; those who had not heard of

the drama being enacted in their midst came simply to congratulate, and those who had came to offer sympathy or more often than not out of curiosity. Mr. Graily called briefly, sent by the Prince to inquire after Signor Pucci. Among the great number of flowers delivered was a single crimson rose in a silver holder. Marissa took it and placed it beside her bed so that it might be the last thing she saw before she slept and the first to greet her when she awoke.

One of the callers on that first morning was Sir Hugo Severin. He came early and seemed somewhat brusque in manner. Marissa attributed this to a recollection of his behavior at the ball and, for Cosmo's sake, went out of her way to set him at ease. It was not possible for him to see Cosmo, she explained apologetically. He was now conscious, but still much too ill to be allowed callers.

"I do understand," he said, still with some stiffness. "Your friend Egerton made the situation very plain to me last evening."

Since Marissa knew nothing of the altercation at the theater, she was completely mystified, but because they were much indebted to him, and Cosmo, in particular, seemed to have a high regard for him, she subdued her natural instincts and assured him that he should see her cousin the moment Sir James gave his consent.

There followed an awkward little silence when it seemed as though he would say more. "Marissa . . ." he began urgently.

At that moment Celestine and Rupert were announced. Sir Hugo's lips tightened angrily. He made a leg and begged to be excused, and the two men passed in the doorway with barely concealed hostility.

"Rupert, whatever did you say last night to put Sir Hugo in such a pucker?" Marissa demanded of him.

Rupert grinned sheepishly and gave her the gist of what had passed between them. "Well, you surely can't pretend you'd have wanted him interfering in your affairs?"

Marissa said no, but she'd as lief not have him upset. A small worried crease marred her brow.

"I say! You don't really like Severin?"

Marissa shuddered slightly. "Oh, no! But Cosmo does, I think."

"Then he will return. The thickness of that man's skin is quite unbelievable!"

As the days passed, Marissa insisted upon taking her turn with the nursing so that Tia Giannina should not wear herself out. This meant that with her remaining theater commitments she was less able to go out. Perry insisted that he did not mind and would willingly forego a few parties, though there was to be a most splendid Venetian breakfast arranged out at Merton upon the following weekend, if she should be able to get away.

Marissa thought it unlikely, but she encouraged him to attend this and other late-Season affairs without her. From both Celestine and Kitty she learned that he had several times been seen talking to Sally Morton. At Almack's last evening, Kitty confided with conspiratorial relish, he had even managed to solicit her hand for the cotillion in spite of Mama's efforts to separate them.

"I believe Lady Morton has her eye on Cheam as a prospective husband for Sally. At all events, she was more than usually ingratiating on the one occasion I have seen them together!"

"Oh, but . . . she would not do *that* to her own daughter, surely?" Marissa was horrified. "The Marquis has a dreadful reputation!"

Kitty sighed. "I know. But he is also in the market for a rich wife—and as soon as may be. And only think how her ladyship would gloat to have her daughter a marchioness!"

Marissa was quite genuinely shocked—and worried. She had met Sally only briefly, but the thought of that delightful child in Cheam's hands was not to be borne! And all because of her, for if she had not encouraged Perry, Sally's future would not now be in question. It must not be!

"Does Perry know of Lady Morton's designs?"

"Oh, I shouldn't think so, although he must learn of it before long if Lord Cheam's attentions grow much more marked."

Then he must be made aware, Marissa decided.

It was a tribute to her popularity that even when the theater closed for the summer, and many of the regular visitors to Arlington Street left for the country or for Brighton or other similar but less fashionable watering places, those who remained in Town continued to call. Any hopes that Marissa might have entertained about moving out of London must now be held in abeyance; the likelihood of Signor Pucci's being fit enough to travel was a remote one. However, Mrs. Arbuthnot had very kindly suggested that as soon as Sir James considered the signor to be strong enough, he should go to her Chiswick house to begin his recuperation.

"I'm off on one of my little jaunts next week, so it's yours for as long as you please, m'dear," she told Marissa. "Your cousin can have a day bed out on the terrace and walk a little in the garden when he gets stronger. How does that sound?"

"It sounds marvelous! I do not know how to thank you!" said Marissa.

"Oh, I don't want thanks. You'll be doing me a favor"—there was a glint in Mrs. Arbuthnot's eye—"stop my servants growing idle!"

Gervase approved the idea. He called every day,

163

usually at a time when he might best find her alone. Quite often he would sit with Signor Pucci, alone or in company with Marissa, talking quietly to the invalid in a way that demanded nothing in return by way of conversation. These visits did Cosmo so much good that, even were she not falling more in love with each day that passed, she must have been deeply grateful to him. As it was, she radiated happiness to such an extent that it was marked by all who came in contact with her. To those who did not know of Mr. Maxwell's frequent visits, it was attributed to her joy at Signor Pucci's recovery.

But Tia Giannina was not so easily fooled. She had noted the rose beside Marissa's bed, also the look in her eyes when Mr. Maxwell was near.

"Do not suppose that my wits have grown dull with so much time spent in the sick room," she scoffed when Marissa balked at her seemingly innocent observation that some people might find it odd, the way her hand was given to one gentleman when her heart so clearly belonged to another! She had watched with satisfaction the wild tide of color that flooded into Marissa's face.

"*Oh, please,* dear Tia Giannina, do not ask me to explain. You shall know all as soon as I am free to speak, I promise you!"

But the old lady had all the answer she needed. "Did I ask for explanations?" She was majestically cryptic as she swept from the room. "Me—I know! In matters of the heart, it was ever thus!"

Sir Hugo Severin had also been watching Marissa with some curiosity; ever solicitous for Signor Pucci's well-being, ever seeking for an opportunity to be alone with Marissa, he was not an easy man to dissuade. The more he was resisted, the more persistent he became.

The day finally arrived when he left Signor Pucci's

room, and upon his inquiring for the signorina, a new young footman, who had not been primed to deny her presence to Sir Hugo, ushered him into the drawing room where she was found seated at the pianoforte, going over one of her songs for a forthcoming concert—and quite alone.

Marissa had an immediate sensation of being trapped, but since she could hardly show him the door, she must perforce swallow her irritation and beg him with forced politeness to be seated. He did so, uttering the usual platitudes about Cosmo and how marked was the improvement since his last visit.

He said with that cool air of partiality which always made her feel so uncomfortable, "My dear, do not, I beg of you, let me take you from your work. To hear you sing always gives me the greatest pleasure."

But she turned her back on the music and folded her hands. He made polite conversation for a few minutes and she replied mechanically, her mind drifting occasionally to wonder when they might move to Chiswick; perhaps, once they were installed there, Sir Hugo would call less often.

She came to with a sense of horror to hear him saying with restrained passion, "I can remain silent no longer. It is absurd that you should continue to pay lip service to a betrothal that was forced upon you. Young Marlow can neither match your brilliance nor be of the least use to you in your work." His tone was scathing. "And as it is clear that your cousin will be incapable of protecting you or furthering your singing for some considerable time, if ever again . . ."

"Sir Hugo!" Marissa sprang to her feet, unable to contain her tongue any longer. "I am not sure what it is you are suggesting, but I beg you will not proceed!"

After a moment he too rose, watching her agitation with odious complacency. "Oh, come! You cannot, I think, be unaware of my regard for you—the interest I have taken in your profession must speak for itself."

"No!" Marissa put out her hands as though she would stop him. "You must not continue . . . you are quite mistaken!"

Sir Hugo crossed the space between them and took her shoulders in a steely clasp. "Am I! Yet I venture to think that such a union would have Signor Pucci's blessing."

He made it sound vaguely like a threat. She was suddenly still.

"You have said nothing to him?"

"As yet, no. In the circumstances I naturally wished to speak to you first. We do not want to disappoint him, do we?"

Marissa's mind was racing; if Cosmo was upset in his present state, it could prove fatal. "You must give me time t-to think," she said.

"Naturally," he said, dry-voiced. His hands slid possessively down her arms to lift her fingers to his lips, his eyes mocking her. "But not too long, I trust!"

When Sir Hugo had gone she tried to think calmly. Everything was becoming so confused. Her immediate instinct was to lay it all before Gervase—but no, in this matter she must find her own solution. Her feet took her without conscious volition into Cosmo's room. The day was warm and the muslin curtains billowed gently as the door opened.

Tia Giannina was straightening the bed covers. She looked up as Marissa entered. "If you are staying, you will sit quietly and not disturb the Maestro! Sir Hugo has already been here, filling his head with talk of tours and concerts and the like." She sniffed her disapproval. "I shall go to make him one of my restorative infusions." At the door she turned. "And kindly do not disarrange that bed!"

Marissa glanced at Cosmo and he lifted a capricious eyebrow; it was the merest parody of his former self, but it was so good to see that she giggled with childish relief. He did look better, she decided, looking more intently at him. A day or two since he had been as white as the pillows that now supported him, and in his delirium he had called her Rosa. Today Luigi had shaved him and there was a trace of color in the aquiline face. It was the eyes that most betrayed his weakness—and his hands, now thinner and more heavily veined than ever, trembled very slightly as they lay upon the silk-embroidered quilt. He patted the place beside him on the wide expanse of bed.

"Do not regard Tia Giannina," he said invitingly, each word still an effort.

Like a delinquent child she settled herself gleefully at his side, feet drawn up, and sighed. "It *is* peaceful in here."

"Dear me. Is it then not so elsewhere?"

Marissa shrugged, remembered that she must not worry him, and fell to plucking at the quilt.

"You should get out more," he ventured. "Does your Lord Marlowe not wish to take you out?"

"He is not mine! At least—" Again she made a dismissive kind of gesture. "I do not care to go with Perry." She looked up, frowning fiercely. "Besides, I don't want to be away from you until you are stronger."

A quiver of emotion disturbed the finely etched features. "That . . . is flattering, child, but foolish. I shall speak to Mr. Maxwell when he comes. Maybe his argument will have more influence than mine."

A wild tide of color suffused her face. He watched it with interest. "So!" he said softly. "Sits the wind in that quarter?" His mouth quirked. "And I thought he came so regularly out of solicitude for my health!"

"You wouldn't mind?" she asked, looking anxiously

for the least sign of disturbance in his face, but if he had misgivings, he kept them well hidden.

"*Cara mia*—all I want is for you to be happy. Signor Maxwell is a gentleman for whom I have great respect. If he pleases you, then I could not wish for better."

Marissa fell to plucking at the quilt again. "There *is* one thing. He does love me, of that I am sure, but—he has not mentioned . . . that is, I don't think he wishes to marry me . . . ?"

His answer surprised her. "And is that *so* important if he truly loves you?"

She looked up at him, wondering. "You are quite right, of course. A little while ago I thought it was dreadfully important! Now, I only know that I want to be with him."

"Then that is how it should be," he said, looking suddenly frail and very weary.

"I have exhausted you!" she exclaimed, scrambling off the bed and frantically straightening the covers again. "Tia Giannina will skin me alive!"

He smiled faintly. "I won't let her. But I think I will rest now."

"Can I stay? I will sit here in the chair and not say another word."

When Tia Giannina came in presently bearing his restorative drink, he was asleep and Marissa was sitting by the window, gazing out with a faraway look in her eyes.

Lord Marlowe was suffering from a severe oppression of the spirit, an affliction which a visit to Vauxhall Gardens in the company of Charlie Hallam and his friends had done little to alleviate. With the end of July in sight, London had grown sadly flat, as well as being stuffy and faintly odorous, and with most of his own particular friends already enjoying life in the more invigorating air of Brighton, there was hardly anyone at Vauxhall that he knew. When Charlie presently exhorted him to join in the dancing which was going forth in the rotunda, he declined, preferring to remain alone in their booth, drinking steadily, a prey to his thoughts.

It would have been different if Marissa had accompanied him. He had asked her, but she had prevaricated as usual, and, as usual, he seemed to lack the power to sway her. He adored her, of course, but he sometimes wished she would treat him less as though he were incapable of mature reasoning.

"I am sorry to disappoint you, my dear," she had said only that morning when he presumed to argue, "but you do understand that I cannot possibly leave Tia Giannina to shoulder the whole burden of nursing Cosmo?"

"If you say so, dearest." His answer was grudging. "Though, I do think—well, it don't seem fitting that you should have to wear yourself out in this way when you might easily bring in a nurse."

"Some dreadful gin-drinking slattern?" She had been almost short with him. "As if I would! Besides, it is not a question of *having* to, Perry—I very much *wish* to do my share in nursing Cosmo. He has given many years of his life to promoting my interests . . . a poor thing it would be if I begrudged him a little of my time now when he needs me."

Faced with such a forceful argument, there was little more he could say without appearing insensitive. But with his ego already severely bruised from having received that morning a blistering missive from his father, he came as near to being out of charity with her as he had ever been.

A severe attack of the gout had mercifully prevented Lord Weare from posting to London immediately upon receiving the news of the engagement, but the exigencies of his condition had, if anything, lent an added touch of originality to his spleenetic diatribe, in which his son and heir was condemned as "a skitter-brained, good-for-nothing jackanapes, a damned moon-calf whose prattling on about love was only fit to turn bile!" There was much more in a similar vein much of it concerning his treatment of the Mortons. The letter concluded with the exhortation that he should come to his senses before any lasting harm was done.

The only part of his papa's letter which made any impression upon him, other than a profound relief that so much distance separated them, was the reference to Sally Morton. Perry could not rid himself of the notion, put into his head so unwittingly by Marissa, that Sally cared deeply for him. He had seen quite a lot of Sally in these past few days and though she was a little more withdrawn than he was used to, her manner toward him seemed very much the same as it had ever been. Yet he was troubled, for only last evening, he had heard the astonishing rumor that Lord Cheam was showing a decided interest in her, and the emotions that this aroused in his breast were, to say the least, confusing. He could not believe that her parents would permit such a match, but Lord Morton so seldom left his estate in Gloucestershire that he was perhaps unaware of Cheam's unsavory reputation.

The sound of laughter roused Perry from his musing. In the booth opposite, a large family group were enjoying themselves prodigiously, and he saw that the both next to it, which had been empty, was now occupied. It gave him something of a shock to see Sally, of all people, seated near the front of it, with none other than Cheam leaning down to address some remark to her. At the rear of the booth, Lady Morton sat, wafting a fan slowly back and forth and watching the couple with what seemed to him to be a quite shocking degree of complacency. It was not difficult, even at a distance, to see how Sally shrank from the odious intimacies of the Marquis, and Perry surprised in himself a very strong urge to go charging across there and plant Cheam a leveler!

As it was, he sat glowering at the booth opposite until, as though the very force of his grievance had made itself felt, Sally looked up and saw him. In that unguarded instant her eyes betrayed her innermost feelings so clearly that she might as well have cried aloud for his help. But what was he to do? Her mama's presence was an insurmountable obstacle and he could see no way of circumventing her unless Sally herself supplied the opportunity. This she accomplished by making a request of the Marquis. He, looking less than happy, spoke to her ladyship who nodded graciously. Then Sally stood up and allowed Lord Cheam to escort her from the booth across the open space between the booths where the orchestra played and people strolled about in the evening air, in the direction of the rotunda. Perry, too, left his place and followed them.

The rotunda proved to be a popular venue with any number of people dancing or standing about watching. Perry had lost sight of Sally for the moment, but Charlie Hallam, hailing him from across the floor, invited him over, glad to see that he had changed his mind. Perry shook his head, however, and made his way doggedly past a group of loud, overdressed women who called out after him. He saw Sally and Lord Cheam, the latter with obvious reluctance, making up a set for a cotillion with several strangers. Perry swallowed his pride, and turning, seized the hand of one of the women who had followed him a little way and rushed her into the vacant place beside Sally.

171

During the course of the dance, he and Sally came together, and she managed to whisper, "Can you meet me early tomorrow morning—*please*, Perry, at about eight o'clock near the ranger's hut in Green Park?" He signified assent, alarmed by the look in her eyes.

It took him some considerable time to shake off the jade whom he had accosted in such a cavalier fashion; in the end he was obliged to buy refreshments for her, and entertain her until such time as the firework display was underway, when her attention was otherwise engaged for just sufficient time to enable him to slip away.

He was in Green Park well before the appointed hour, pacing restlessly, having hardly closed his eyes all night. His man, who was used to him sleeping until ten o'clock at the very least, was convinced that something must be seriously amiss, the more so when his young master donned breeches and riding coat and departed without uttering a single word of complaint.

Sally was a few minutes late and came running over the grass with some of the hoydenish grace of the old Sally. "Oh, Perry, I am *so* glad you are here!" she cried and, to his dismay, burst into tears. The next instant she was in his arms, and somehow, in the course of comforting her, of straightening her bonnet and mopping up her tears, declaring that, whatever it was that was making her so very unhappy, he would put it right, Perry made a shattering discovery. This dear, pliant creature in his arms, whom he had known for so long that he had taken her for granted, meant everything to him.

He cupped her chin tenderly in his hand and said in a rather dazed way, "Oh, Sally, I *do* love you!" And then he kissed her and she responded in a way that left no doubt in either of their minds about her feelings for him.

It was Sally who was the first to pull away. She said shakily, "Oh, Perry, we must not! You are not free."

Belatedly, he remembered Marissa. "Oh, Lord!" he groaned. "What a devilish predicament!"

"You cannot forswear her! She is so lovely . . . and generous, and . . . oh . . ."

"But I don't love her! I thought I did, but I don't! I love you! I think I must always have loved you, but I couldn't see it!" Perry clenched his fists, and said, frowning, "Well, there is nothing for it—I shall have to explain to her. She will understand . . ."

"You can't!" Sally said, making an effort to be brave. "Oh, dear, I should never have asked you to come."

"What nonsense!" Perry looked at her closely, still frowning. "Why did you, by the way?"

She gave an endearing sniff and scrubbed determinedly at her eyes. "Well, the thing is, Mama has accepted an invitation for us to stay at th-the Marquis of Cheam's house in Sussex. W-we are supposed to leave tomorrow and Mama says that I shall be on trial and that if the Marquis approves my behavior, he will offer for m-me!" Two large fresh tears filled her eyes and brimmed over. "I'm s-sorry to be so feeble, Perry, but I just couldn't bear to marry that man!"

"I should think not, indeed!" he exclaimed, adding with dawning resolution, "Nor shall you, by Jove!"

"Well, I had hoped that if I could get back to tell Papa he would say I didn't have to . . ." she explained. "And I have wondered if you would be so good as to take me home?"

"That's easy enough," he said, "but can you be sure he will take your part?"

Sally's confidence wilted slightly. "I don't *think* he would make me do something so very much against

173

my will, even though it is Mama who usually has the say . . ."

Perry was very conscious of the weight of responsibility now resting upon him. "Look here," he said. "I don't think we should do anything in a hurry. What we must do is hide you away somewhere for a day or two—until we decide."

"But where? I have thought and thought, and there is nowhere I can go!"

His first thought was of Kitty, but she might feel in conscience bound to notify Lord Morton—or worse still, Lady Morton.

And then he had it. "I know the very place!" he cried. "And it is the very last place anyone will think to look for you!" And, as she gazed adoringly up at him: "Marissa will hide you!"

Chapter 13

Sally stared at him, her tears forgotten. "Perry, you cannot treat Signorina Merrilli so shabbily! Why, I must be the very last person she will wish to shelter when she learns that it is I who am to take you from her! You really cannot expect otherwise."

Perry seemed much struck by her reasoning. but after a moment's consideration, he shook his head. "No, Marissa ain't one to take the huff. She's the very best of good sorts—not a mean bone in her! And as for her feelings—well, the more I consider it, the less certain I am that she is in love with me . . ."

"Oh, but how could she not be?"

"I don't know. I certainly thought it to be so, though she was ever teasing me. Perhaps I wanted to think it! But just recently, ever since our engagement, in fact, she has been—oh, I don't know—different, almost offhand."

"But did you not say that she has been much distressed by her cousin's illness?"

"Yes, but it is more than that." Perry thrust out his chin decisively. "Anyhow, we must take that chance, and what is more, we must act now, for I'll tell you something else. I don't believe you should go back to Lady Chessborough's. Your mama might twig something is afoot! Best if you just disappear."

"Oh, I don't think—" Sally frowned earnestly. "Well, quite apart from the dreadful prospect of arriving upon the signorina's doorstep with only what I am wearing, only consider how Mama will worry if I leave her no word."

Perry began to laugh, and as her chin rose indignantly and she demanded to know what was so funny, he took her in his arms, pushed the bonnet back from her face, and kissed away her objections. "Oh, Sal, I adore you!"

She found this very much more to her liking and it was quite some moments before he was able to assert with his newfound confidence, "I am sorry to have to say it, but your mama will be well served! Only trust me, my love, and I will bring you safe through it all."

"Very well," she agreed shyly.

Marissa sang softly to herself as she dressed, and Maria, helping her into a flimsy gown of pale cream muslin and brushing her hair and catching it back from her face with a pearl clasp, thought that it was some time since she had seen her mistress so happy. She suspicioned that it had something to do with Mr. Maxwell who had now become such a regular visitor, for was it not the same Mr. Maxwell who had caused her so much heartache earlier in the summer?

There was indeed a kind of light-headedness about the way Marissa felt; a polite regretful note had been penned and dispatched to Sir Hugo on the previous day, thanking him for the honor, etcetera, and hoping that her refusal of his offer would not alter in any way his friendship with Signor Pucci. She was most careful to stress that her decision had been taken with Signor Pucci's full knowledge and consent so that he would not come bothering Cosmo about it. Now it remained only to persuade Perry that he did not in the least wish to marry her, and she would be free to give herself to Gervase.

So it was in ebullient mood that she floated down the stairs just as Signora Tortinallo was crossing the lower landing. The old lady found herself seized by her immense waist and twirled exuberantly around.

"Mother of God! Let be, will you?" she panted, struggling to free herself. "Such behavior! Do you wish my head to spin?"

"Oh, but is it not a beautiful morning, *cara mia?*" Marissa crooned at her.

"For some, no doubt it is so," agreed the old lady dryly, straightening her skirts. "Easy to tell who it is that works in this house and who does not."

"That is unjust, but I shall not regard it. I am in charity with the whole world this morning! How is the Maestro? May I go in to him?"

"Certainly not." The signora was uncompromisingly stern. "Luigi is only now assisting him with his ablutions, and besides, in your present mood, you will wear him to a thread before the day is begun!"

Downstairs, the doorknocker sounded imperatively.

"Then I shall take a walk," Marissa decided. "In the Park, I think. What a pity we do not own a dog—a dog would enjoy to run in the Park on such a morning, don't you agree?"

Signora Tortinallo looked at her closely, and sniffed. "I hope that you are not sickening for a fever."

Marissa laughed, and was about to go back for her hat when she heard the sound of voices in the hall. Hoping that it might be Gervase, she leaned over the banister rail, not heeding Tia Giannina's reproving "tuts." But it was Perry who came into view and there was someone with him—she caught a glimpse of sprig muslin, a slight, youthful figure . . .

"You *are* early, Perry," she called to him. "And Miss Morton, also. What a pleasant surprise! Do come along up, both of you."

In the drawing room she turned to face her visitors. Miss Morton, with her fair curls tumbling in unruly fashion from an inexpertly tied bonnet, was flushed, a little breathless—and nervous. Perry was equally ill-at-ease. They both looked terribly young, and riddled with guilt, and as they each cast a swift glance at the other as if to draw strength and comfort, it was not difficult to divine the reason.

"We are not *too* early?" gasped Miss Morton.

"We can come back later," offered Perry, grasping, she thought, at straws.

"No, no. Pray do be seated." The knowledge that they were going to make things easy for her filled Marissa with elation; she had known from the moment the birds had awakened her that it was going to be that kind of day. Perry, having seated himself momentarily, had risen again and was pacing the floor, nerving himself to begin. She might have helped him, but some imp of mischief made her fold her hands and wait. In spite of his nervousness she sensed a new maturity about him, and it would do him no harm, after all, to prove himself before this child who looked at him with such adoring eyes.

"Marissa, there is a favor we wish to ask of you, but first . . ." He faltered, and as both young ladies silently willed him to go on, he began again with renewed determination. "I have something to say to you and I don't expect you to think other than badly of me, for I don't think well of myself—only it is frightfully important, you see . . ."

"It is all my fault, ma'am," Sally broke in, trying to help him.

"No it isn't," he retorted bravely. "Sally would have sacrificed her own feelings, but, you see, we have discovered that we love one another, and something has happened which—in short, she does need my support quite desperately. And so, if you would consent to release me from our engagement . . ."

Marissa, though very much conscious of how much

178

such a confession must have cost him, could not but find the scene hugely diverting—a librettist could not devise a better tragi-comedy! If only it could be set to music, it would play to full houses every night. She sprang up and tottered to the center of the room, her arm thrown up to shield her eyes.

"My God!" she cried, in recitative. "I am betrayed!"

They looked at her and then at each other in alarm. Perry took a step toward her, his face white and tense. "Marissa . . ." he began.

"Oh, who will succor me?" Her shoulders shaking by now, Marissa could not continue. She lowered her arm and they saw that she was laughing. "Oh, foolish children! You surely did not think me *so* poor-spirited? My poor Perry, if you only knew! I have been in a positive quake for fear of wounding *you!*"

Miss Morton was so astonished that she could only sit, the color gradually coming back into her face as Perry and the signorina fell upon each other in mutual relief. Perry mopped his eyes and looked a trifle sheepish.

"You know, I could not help feeling that your affections were not wholly engaged," he said, grinning. "But it is very bad of me, just the same and I do not blame you for roasting me! Only, you see—" He explained about the Marquis of Cheam and how frightened Sally was. "And that was when I realized, you understand?"

"But, of course! I can quite see how it was, and you were quite right to act as you did." Marissa turned to Sally who was by now recovered from her fright. "My dear Miss Morton, Perry has shown great sense in bringing you to me," she said approvingly. "You may stay here for as long as it takes Perry to make arrangements for your journey." As Sally stood up to thank her, Marissa eyed her trim little figure. "I am rather taller than you, I fear, but I am sure we can

179

soon make some dresses over to fit you until you are able to recover your own." She held out a hand. "Come, and my Maria shall see what she can do. There are several very pretty lawns—one in jonquil yellow that should become you especially well . . ."

She turned to bid Perry make himself comfortable and he grasped her other hand and assured her a trifle incoherently that he was deeply grateful for the generosity she had shown them, and when she pooh-poohed this, he broached the delicate question of how best to terminate their engagement officially.

"Perhaps you will permit me to send an announcement to the *Gazette?*"

"By all means," she replied cordially. "Do whatever seems best to you." She smiled mischievously. "What a pity so many of our friends have gone away—we could have held a party and had the most terrible quarrel in public. It would have been such fun!"

Gervase, too, had been occupied in setting his house in order. Miss Wellam had been given her *congé*, very firmly but kindly—her distress considerably alleviated by his handsome parting gift of a gleaming new lady's phaeton with a beautifully behaved little black mare between the shafts.

"Honestly, Gervase, you are much too generous!" Kitty said reprovingly when he called in at Hill Street to give her the news. "I don't doubt that Miss Wellam will be the richer by more than a phaeton! I know for a fact that she had that diamond necklace from you only a month or two back, and goodness knows how many other expensive trinkets!"

"But then," he explained apologetically, "I must needs salve my conscience where poor Perdita is concerned, for I made rather shameful use of her."

Kitty looked at him curiously. He had caught her in the throes of packing for the family's journey into the country, an exercise that had driven Edward to seek refuge at White's, but all thought of packing had been forgotten with the arrival of Gervase.

"We had wondered," she said ingenuously. "Edward remarked most particularly that Miss Wellam wasn't at all in your usual style, and I must say that I am vastly relieved that you are rid of her." She eyed him critically; he was looking particularly well, she thought, from his gleaming hessians and pale fawn pantaloons to the restrained elegance of his cravat, and there was a gleam in his eye that did not accord in the least particular with a man in the throes of ending a relationship.

She sighed. "Dear Gervase," she said pensively. "I do wish you might find someone very special—someone with whom you might contemplate spending the rest of your life."

Gervase looked at Kitty for several moments without answering. It was with a slight pang that he was, in a sense, bidding farewell to that ephemeral flower of his youth who had never until now been surpassed; he would always cherish a particular affection for Kitty, but that special place in his heart which had for so long been reserved for that little ghost of memory was now occupied by a flesh-and-blood creature of whose delights he would never tire.

His long sensitive mouth was cursed into a faint smile as he murmured, "Then it would seem, my dear Kitty, that your wish is about to be fulfilled."

"Gervase!" she squeaked, holding out her hands to him. "You are—yes, I do believe you are in love—really in love at last! Oh, do tell me, who is she? Do I know her?"

"Very well, I think. But I must crave your discretion, my dear, for I have not yet asked her to be my wife, though I have every reason to believe she will accept me . . ."

"Gervase!" Kitty cried. "Oh, you infuriating man, I shall die of curiosity if you do not tell me at once! I won't breathe a word, even to Edward, if you do not wish it, but I must know!"

His eyebrow quirked expressively. "It is Marissa."

She stared at him for a moment and then her face lit up. "But of course! She is exactly right for you! Oh, how sly you are to have said nothing until now!"

"I am naturally delighted that you approve," he said whimsically.

When Gervase left Hill Street he drove to the offices of his solicitor and thereafter to Arlington Street. As he drew up before Marissa's door a shabby figure detached itself from the railings and sloped off around the corner. His behavior might have gone unnoticed had Gervase not remembered having seen him before in similar circumstances. On an impulse he whipped up the horses and gave chase. The youth moved swiftly, but he was no match for a curricle and pair.

Gervase passed him, brought the curricle smartly to a halt, and tossing the ribbons to Wyatt, his groom, sprang down. The youth saw him and made to dart across the road, but before he had gone more than a few yards he found himself held in a bruising grip very much at odds with his adversary's appearance.

"Leave off, guv!" he begged. "I ain't done nothing, as God's my judge!"

"Profaning your Maker, lad?" Gervase had the youth's arm pinned behind him in such a way that it would hurt only if he struggled. He was tall and incredibly thin, the wrist now firmly in his hold being nothing but bone and sinew—but his bright blue eyes showed that he did not want for intelligence. "The innocent don't usually have cause to run away!"

"No, well—I was tryin' to pluck up me courage, see?—to knock at the door. I have been for days now."

The youth wriggled uncomfortably and winced. "I come, you see, just like she said I was to do . . ."

"She?"

"Miss Merrilli, guv. A regular trump, she is, and nō mistake!" said the boy with a brave show of jauntiness. 'You just come along to see me, Elijah,' she says, 'if ever you falls on hard times'—so come I did."

"Elijah?" queried Gervase, one eyebrow quirking irrepressibly, then he grew stern once more. "Coming it a bit brown, aren't you, lad?"

"I'm telling the truth!" Elijah insisted. "Look, if you'll just leave go . . ."

"Oh-ho no! I didn't come up with the grass, young Master Elijah! I loose my hold and you'll be off like a jack-rabbit!"

"I won't, honest! I've got a paper she give me, see? If you won't take my say-so, you've only to put a hand in my pocket. There—see?" Gervase, intrigued, took out the grimy slip of paper containing the address. "In her own hand, that is"—there was a certain awe in his voice which quickly gave way to truculence—"as you'll likely know if you're a friend of hers!"

Gervase could not but admire the boy's spirit. "Very well, my lad," he said. "We will go and see Signorina Merrilli together."

He signaled to Wyatt, who had been keeping a close eye on the proceedings ready to intervene if necessary, and told him to walk the horses. Then he released his hold on the boy. "Don't try anything," he advised softly and was treated to a swift pugnacious grin.

"G'arn!" said Elijah loftily, smoothing down the sleeve of his shabby out-at-the-wrist coat. "Wivout yer bleedin' curricle, I could outrun you any day of the week!"

As Gervase could scarcely refute this assertion, he

wisely refrained from comment, but his lips twitched briefly. When the door was opened to them, he stood aside and pushed the boy in before him.

Marissa was just coming downstairs. Her face lit up with joy upon seeing him, and then, seeing that he was not alone, "Why, whatever . . . ?" She ran down the remaining stairs and recognized his companion. "Heavens! It is Elijah Briggs!"

"There!" said Elijah triumphantly. "I told you, didn't I?" He turned back to Marissa with a certain diffidence. "You did say to come, miss, if I couldn't get no work?"

"Yes, of course I did!" She caught a quizzical look from Gervase and colored quite charmingly. "Elijah and I met at the theater," she explained in a rush just as Signora Tortinallo came from the kitchen quarters below and, seeing Elijah, waddled purposefully across the hall.

"What does this mean? Signorina Marissa, why does that ingrate come here—and how?"

"I told him to."

The signora threw up her hands. "I knew it! Did I not foretell how it would be? A stone about your neck."

"Nonsense," said Marissa firmly, giving the boy an encouraging smile. "Elijah is going to be very useful to me."

"Doing what? I ask you—first it is a young lady who comes secretly to hide herself away, without so much as a handkerchief for baggage—"

Gervase shot a quick interested glance at Marissa; she was nibbling furiously at her lower lip, the very picture of guilt.

"—and now we have this . . . tatterdemalion"—the signora was well into her stride—"who should be languishing in prison, where he assuredly belongs, were it not for a certain crazy-headed opera singer who

wished to play God! So, I ask myself, who do we succor next? Perhaps we should ask in the man who
sweeps the street?"

"You are being quite ridiculous, Tia Giannina, and
you know it," said Marissa hurriedly. "Now, please be
so good as to arrange for Elijah to be taken down to
the kitchens where chef is to give him food." Again
she smiled at the boy, who looked uneasy. "I will see
you later and we will decide upon your duties." She
added, *sotta voce*, "Take no notice of the signora's
tongue. She does not mean half that she says!"

The boy was led reluctantly away to the accompa-
niment of much muttering, and Marissa and Gervase
went upstairs, not to the drawing room but to a small-
er salon to the rear of the landing.

"We should not go into the drawing room just at
present," she confided in conspiratorial tones, closing
the door. "At least, I think Perry would not welcome
us, and anyway, we could not be private."

Gervase threw his hat on to a chair and without
preamble took her in his arms and kissed her in a
very thorough fashion.

"Why did you do that?" she inquired dreamily
when at last he lifted his head.

He looked down at her in some amusement. "Do I
have to have a reason?"

She shook her head, dimpling, and reached up a
proprietory hand to touch the silver in his hair; he
caught the hand and pressed a kiss into the palm.
"Then let us simply call it a salute to a crazy-headed
opera singer who also happens to be my very beautiful, desirable, and maddeningly mysterious love!"

Marissa laughed delightedly. "Come and sit down
and I will explain everything to you."

And there on the sofa, with one of his arms around
her and his free hand covering hers as they lay
clasped on her knee, she told him briefly how Elijah

185

had come into her life and then hurried on to the news about Perry. "It was clever of me, I think, to make him take notice of Sally. But even I did not suppose that they would rediscover one another so soon!"

"And Perry is to send an announcement to the *Gazette*?" Gervase was watching her intently. She turned and met his eyes a little shyly.

"Yes. So you see, there is nothing now to impede us—except perhaps that I should wait until Cosmo recovers more fully before I can contemplate leaving. I have told him, by the way, about us ..."

Gervase chuckled. "You have been busy!"

"Yes, and he is most pleased. I told him also that you did not wish to marry me ..."

"The devil you did!"

"Well, but I thought that he should know—and he understands perfectly! He says that it is not *so* important so long as we are truly in love, and I agree with him!"

"You do?" His eyebrow was wildly quizzical.

"Of course. I had already come to that conclusion, only it seemed at the time that you were taking me for granted, and so I ..."

He stopped her mouth with kisses before she could proceed further. "I am put to shame, my darling! It is a great wonder to me that you should wish to have anything to do with such an insensitive, conceited looby!"

Marissa giggled. "You are not *so* bad, and indeed, I would not have you any different!"

"Well, that is a great pity, for I am resolved upon reform. From this moment all shall be as you wish, though for my part, I had rather set my heart upon marriage! I have discovered, you see, that it will take me no less than a lifetime to love you the way I mean to love you." The mockery was gone, to be replaced

186

by an intense, almost pleading seriousness. "And to that end, my dearest Marissa, I should be proud and honored to have you for my wife."

She was trembling, her mind in a whirl. "If you really mean it . . . if you are not just doing this for my sake, for indeed you need not . . ."

"I never meant anything more."

"Then, of course I will marry you!" Her eyes, very large and unnaturally brilliant, lifted to him. "Oh, Gervase, *mio carissimo*, I am dreadfully afraid I am going to cry! I almost always do when I am deliriously happy!"

But he gave her no time to think of tears and it was very much later when he said at last, "Do you think, my love, that Signor Pucci is sufficiently recovered to sustain a visit from me, so that I may make a formal request for your hand?"

She sighed blissfully. "I expect so, but we had better ask Tia Giannina."

"Must we!" he groaned. "I have the feeling that woman would crush me underfoot without a qualm."

"Oh, no!" Marissa giggled. "You are very much in her good books since you saved her beloved Maestro's life."

"I doubt that I did *so* much, but if it pleases her to think it, then life will at least lose one of its terrors!"

"Nonsense!" Marissa retorted. "There is not a woman born that you could not charm if you had a mind to it!"

"True," he agreed with disarming frankness. "But the signora is not a woman—more likely a she-dragon who would defend her charges to the death if need be!"

The signora, however, offered no objections to his visiting her patient; perhaps the expression in Marissa's eyes was sufficient to reassure her that the news was good, and indeed, so it proved. Signor Pucci was quietly thankful to know that Marissa would have the security of an abiding love.

"I have been much troubled in my mind about her future, Mr. Maxwell. Now, I feel a great weight has been lifted from me." The Maestro was looking a little stronger with each day that passed. He spoke to Gervase as one man of the world to another. "You will have heard many rumors about Marissa and me—" A smile touched the aesthetic features. "They are quite unfounded. She is more as a daughter to me. Yes, a daughter." He paused as though his thoughts were suddenly elsewhere. "Mr. Maxwell, will you bear with me? There is something I would confide to you."

Gervase signified his willingness, but begged that the signor would not feel obliged to tire himself with tedious explanations. One hand lifted off the quilt in a dismissive gesture.

"It is well, perhaps, that you should know, and I believe that you, more than most, will be sympathetic to my predicament." The voice was firmer, stronger than for some days as he began. "It is now more than twenty-five years since I fell in love with Marissa's mother. We were cousins, Rosa and I. She had lived for all of her seventeen years in Milan, whilst I, after much success as a singer, had assumed the mantle of teacher and, occasionally, impresario. It was therefore inevitable that her family should give her into my charge when she began to display a not inconsiderable talent."

The thin voice softened perceptibly as this point and the smile was back, playing about his mouth. "For the first few weeks Rosa fought me at every turn and then came rapport and finally we fell in love." Signor Pucci's heavy eyelids lifted and he regarded Gervase with a certain rueful candor. "There was a considerable difference in age, but when one loves—"

He shrugged. "And then a young Irishman came to Venice—oh, such charm he had, and handsome! He was, without a doubt, feckless, but Rosa could see only what she wished to see. Without a thought she abandoned a promising future, and me, to go with her bold Irishman . . ."

Gervase wondered if he should stop the narrative before Signor Pucci became exhausted, but the thought that perhaps the old man needed to unburden himself to someone held him silent a little longer. And there was no gainsaying that he found the tale intriguing.

"I am nearly done," said the signor as though reading his thoughts. "I heard nothing from Rosa until seven years ago, when I received a letter, scarcely decipherable, to say that she was dying of consumption, and that her husband was already dead. She begged my patronage for her daughter, born seven and a half months after her marriage . . ." Gervase drew in a sharp breath and the eyes of the two men met. "Exactly so, my friend! That was all that she said—perhaps she was not even sure in her own mind—but for me it was enough. I arrived, too late to see Rosa, and took Marissa, then fifteen, back to Venice. Her voice showed even more promise than Rosa's had; she took her mother's last name, and so we began again. I have always treated her as a daughter, though I need hardly say that she is totally ignorant of her history and I would prefer her to remain so." He shrugged. "But, though I trust I shall not quit this world quite yet, it seemed to me that you ought to know."

"I am honored to have been the recipient of your confidence, signor. Marissa shall know nothing of it from me."

"I thank you." Signor Pucci sighed. "It may seem an impertinence to ask one thing more of you, but have you considered how you will feel about Marissa continuing to sing?"

Gervase smiled reassuringly. "My dear Signor Pucci, you need have no fear. It shall be entirely for Marissa to decide. If she wishes to pursue her career, she will have my full support. I cannot hope to emulate you, but I am very willing to learn."

He stood up, seeing the ready tears spring into the other's eyes. "And now, I must go, or I shall be held accountable by Signora Tortinallo!" He took the shakily extended hand in his, his voice gentle. "You will never have cause to regret our marriage, I promise you. And you must get well quickly, for I doubt Marissa will consent to name the day until she knows that you will be at her side!"

Chapter 14

Marissa's days were suddenly very full, and with so much to think about, she hardly noticed the passage of time. Sir James continued to be pleased with Signor Pucci's progress and gave it as his opinion that he would soon be well enough to be moved. He would himself be obliged to return home in a few days, having extended his holiday way beyond its original span, but was happy to leave the signor in the capable hands of a friend and colleague, in whom he had every confidence.

Perry, rapidly increasing in stature by virtue of his new-found responsibility, tired of the inactivity and finally hired a post chaise in order to take Sally home to her father. From Gloucestershire he had written enthusiastically to Marissa concerning the outcome of their journey. Lord Morton had, it seemed, been generous in his forgiveness; so indignant had he been about his daughter's erstwhile plight and his wife's culpability that he had taken a firm stand for once and professed himself happy to bestow Sally's hand upon the son of his oldest friend. Thus Perry had been able to face his own parents with all in a fair way to being settled.

"That boy does have the devil's own cheek, to say nothing of his fickleness!" chuckled Gervase when Marissa showed him the letter. "Not two month's since he was hopelessly enamoured of you, my love.

One can only hope that his feelings will be more enduring where Miss Morton is concerned!"

"They will be," Marissa assured him confidently. "Perry was never really in love with me. He was simply infatuated with the idea of being in love with me!"

"I had no idea that you were so perceptive!" His smile was lazy. "What will you make of my profession of undying adoration, I wonder."

They were sitting on the terrace of the Chiswick house where they had gone to make final arrangements to move there on the following week. It had taken little persuasion on the part of Watts with the promise of cooling drinks to tempt them out onto the terrace where their love had first blossomed and they had lingered long after they might have left.

"You?" Marissa stretched out a hand which he took and held, his generous curving thumb caressing it sensually. She sighed, feeling blissfully indolent and content. "Oh, you are quite a different matter. For you I can see no hope of a reprieve!"

He laughed softly, the pressure of his fingers betraying his delight.

Gervase did not come in with her when they returned to Arlington Street, but she would be meeting him for supper after a concert she was to give that evening.

Marissa went upstairs where she met Elijah coming from the direction of Signor Pucci's room bearing a tray, and looking singularly ill-at-ease in his footman's livery. With his hair ruthlessly brushed into a semblance of order he was almost unrecognizable except for the ready grin which she returned.

He cocked his head back whence he had come. "You got a visitor—or rather the signor has—swell gentry cove!" There was a hint of dislike in his tone, but before she could inquire further, Signora Tortinallo was upon them like an avenging angel.

"How often must I say? The back stairs, and you do not address the signorina in so forward a way! Go!"

He went, shooting an impudent grimace at Marissa as he did so.

"And you should not encourage him! Mother of the Skies! However you could have supposed that this Elijah—such a name!—would ever make a house servant!"

"Well, but at least he is cheerful about the place." Marissa laughed, teasing. "He said something about a visitor, Tia Giannina?"

"Assuredly. It is Sir Hugo Severin. One supposes he must have been from home, so many days it is since he has called!"

The reaction her innocent announcement produced was nothing short of astonishing. *"Dio mio!"* cried Marissa, picking up her skirts. "Is he with the Maestro now?" And without awaiting a reply, she was gone.

She found Cosmo sitting in his chair by the window, looking much more spruce and alert, a rug tucked neatly about him, and facing him, Sir Hugo, one elegant leg crossed over the other, very much at his ease.

He rose upon seeing her, punctilious as ever though his eyes betrayed that he had noted the hasty manner of her entry. It was as though there had been no contention between them; only in his eyes and in the drawling voice did she detect a certain coldness.

"My dear signorina, pray do sit here beside your cousin." She complied, feeling ill at ease as he stood looking down at her. "Permit me to observe how delightfully you are looking—quite blooming, in fact! It is quite apparent that something—this frightful heat

193

perhaps, which most of us find so enervating—agrees with you!"

Marissa made some reply, she knew not what, and willed him to go. But he showed no such willingness to oblige. His flow of polite conversation oppressed her nerves until she felt that she must scream, and knew that he knew it.

"We have had such an interesting talk, Signor Pucci and I, about your future—and other things! I have, I hope, persuaded the signor to allow me to make him the gift of a portrait, Signorina Marissa. I was in the studio of an artist friend of mine only yesterday and found some quite superb sketches he had made of you at the theater."

"It is most kind of Sir Hugo, is it not, Marissa?" Cosmo picked up a small drawing which lay on the table at his elbow. "This one I particularly like." It was a delightful study of her in her costume for *Il Ratto de Cherubins*. "I confess that such a portrait on my wall would give me immense joy when I no longer have you at my side."

Their eyes met, his tinged just a little with melancholy so that her throat ached and she put out a swift, comforting hand. "I shall never be far away while you need me," she promised, and became aware that Sir Hugo's glance moved consideringly from one to the other. But he said nothing.

It was a considerable relief to Marissa when at last he rose to take his leave, expressing the hope that he might be allowed to visit them when they moved to Chiswick.

When the door had closed upon Signor Pucci, however, he said without any appreciable change of tone, "Will you be so good as to afford me a few moments in private with you?" He added, as though anticipating her refusal, "I shall not detain you for long."

Marissa shrugged and took him along to the

drawing room. She made no attempt to sit down, so that he, perforce, must also stand as she confronted him haughtily.

"I must ask you to be brief, Sir Hugo. I have a concert this evening and wish to rest. Since you presumably received my letter, I cannot see that we have anything to say to one another."

He stared down at her, his expression inscrutable, though a tiny muscle twitched spasmodically at the corner of his mouth. "I also read the announcement in the *Gazette*. You and Lord Marlowe are not now to marry?"

"No. We have agreed that we should not suit." Marissa was firm. "But that in no way alters my decision concerning your offer."

His jaw tightened fractionally, but his voice was almost pleasant. "A pity, my dear, because I really do feel that you should seriously reconsider that decision. Signor Pucci is coming along so well. It would be tragic if at this stage he were to suffer a severe setback!"

The thinly veiled threat made her angry; a small knot of fear tightened inside her, though it was not apparent in her manner. "I do not believe that you have the power to hurt Cosmo. He would naturally be a little upset if you withdrew your plans to stage the new opera, but I know he would quickly come to terms with his disappointment, particularly if he knew why you had done so!"

He dismissed her argument with an impatient gesture. "I was not referring to the opera, my dear Marissa, but rather to something of a more . . . personal nature. It concerns the portrait I mean to give to your cousin. My friend, the artist, you see, has a highly developed imagination which, when allied to his natural talent, can produce the most extraordinary results."

Sir Hugo withdrew from an inner pocket a sketch

similar in size to the one he had shown Signor Pucci, and something in the way he looked at it made Marissa's hand tremble slightly as she took it from him. Nothing, however, could have prepared her for the shock she experienced upon seeing the sketch which was of a nude figure lying seductively posed upon a couch, one hand invitingly extended, and in the face, indisputably her face, the artist had captured quite brilliantly all the mischievous allure she had portrayed as Cherubino. Looking at it, her mind went curiously blank.

"Of course, you are not seeing it at its best. The finished portrait is a superb likeness!" Sir Hugo watched her reaction with obvious satisfaction. "It would be unfortunate, would it not, if the signor were to receive the wrong picture by mistake? In his present state of health the shock might even prove fatal!"

Marissa, dry-mouthed, found her voice at last. "You would not . . . ? It would be too cruel!"

"I agree," he said smoothly. "But accidents can happen. Only imagine how dreadful it would be, for instance, if such a picture came to be hung—erroneously, of course—in some quite prominent place!"

This could not really be happening, she thought, as revulsion almost overcame her. "What is it that you want?" she said in a harsh voice hardly recognizable as her own.

His smile was a travesty. "You know what I want, Marissa. I want you. I am even prepared to marry you, which I am sure you will agree, is quite magnanimous of me!"

The insult left her unmoved; in her distraught state she almost blurted out that she couldn't marry him because she was to marry Gervase. Time. She must have time. "When do you want an answer?"

Sir Hugo seemed amused that she should ask; but confidence made him benevolent. "I should have thought that there was only one answer you could give, but I am prepared to humor you." He considered for a moment. "Shall we say tomorrow night? Yes. You know, I have a fancy to play out this little charade in style. There is a small, very secluded house which I am at present occupying on the outskirts of Merton. It is there that the original of the portrait is housed. I will send a carriage for you and you will come to me wearing your rose-colored domino. I, for my part, shall wear my black . . ."

She shuddered, remembering. "It was you, was it not, that evening in Lady Chessington's garden?"

"It was." He inclined his head. "You were a fool to struggle so. I was but trying to save you from discovery—an honor that subsequently fell to another cavalier! This time," he sneered, "I fear that even Maxwell cannot aid you!" Her slow flush spoke more eloquently than words. "You see," he added softly, "I am well aware of your interest in *that* direction, but it would be more than foolish to look for his intervention *this* time."

The sketch was removed from her nerveless clasp and returned to the inside pocket of his coat. He put a finger under her chin, tilting her head. Marissa stiffened, meeting his glance defiantly. "That is much better. I like spirit in a woman. If only you are sensible, we might deal quite well together, you and I—an ideal combination of talents, the perfect partnership, in fact!"

"Never!" she retorted, her eyes flashing with sudden anger.

"We shall see." He gave her cheek a sharp admonitory tap and released her. "Until tomorrow evening, then. Shall we say eight o'clock?"

"I don't know if I can . . ." It was a last despairing throw—and he knew it.

"Oh, you will find a way, I am sure!" He bowed with studied courtesy and strolled to the door.

On the landing he almost fell over a footman bending to retrieve something. There was an undignified moment of scuffling before he regained his balance and with it his authority.

"Out of my way, miserable dolt!" Sir Hugo said through shut teeth as Signora Tortinallo came hurrying into view, full of exclamations. He cut short her apologies. "Oh, let be, ma'am. I advise you to choose your servants with more care! Such gross clumsiness is more fitted to the sweeping of stables!"

He strode angrily toward the stairs and Elijah, stiff-faced, glared at the retreating back. "Aye, cully," he muttered truculently. "And there's a place for you, too—may you find it sooner than you know!"

He scarcely heeded the signora's fierce promise of retribution as she waddled off in Sir Hugo's wake. Marissa had come to see what had happened and, striving to appear no more than concerned for him, inquired if he was all right. But he wasn't fooled. That door hadn't been properly closed during Sir Hugo's visit and he had heard most of what was said. It wasn't prying, he told himself; not really; not when someone as you knew and thought a lot of was being threatened. Elijah hadn't understood all that was said, but he knew intimidation when he heard it and there was a funny, sort of blank look in his Marissa's eyes as he stammered that he was fine and hurried away.

Already in the signora's black books, he braved her wrath still further by slipping into the small saloon, where he shut the door behind him and stood with his back to it as he fished out the paper he had taken from Sir Hugo's inner pocket and stuffed down his breeches; if he was honest with himself, he'd felt a rare spurt of pride upon discovering that he'd not lost

198

his nimble touch—no one would ever believe that that spot of bother was anything but an accident!

He smoothed out the paper, turned it over, and drew in a soundless whistle, his face turning bright scarlet as appreciation turned swiftly to embarrassment. Lord 'a mercy! What was he to do now?

Marissa was beset by a similar dilemma; she could not even consider meeting Sir Hugo's demands just when true happiness with Gervase was within her grasp. Yet she had not the slightest doubt that he would do exactly as he had threatened should she not comply.

Only her years of training enabled her to get through the concert that evening; even so, by the time it was over the strain was beginning to tell. Gervase noticed the change in her immediately, but when after the concert he had suggested canceling the private supper room he had bespoken at Gunter's, she was adamant.

"Tia Giannina will only fuss," she begged him. "A quiet supper will be so much more restful. I daresay it is the heat which has made my head ache a little."

Marissa was very gay over supper but Gervase noticed that, though she drank a great deal, she only toyed with each dish that was laid before her. Finally he gave the order for the covers to be removed. When they were at last alone he came to stand behind her and began to massage her neck as he had done once before. She felt light-headed but his touch did nothing to ease the ache in her heart; that, if anything, grew more intense with the realization that if Sir Hugo had his way, they could never more hope to enjoy moments such as this. Tears constricted her throat and, glancing down at her, Gervase was astonished to see one trickle forlornly down her cheek.

"Marissa?" He came around her chair and crouched

before her, taking her hands in his and begging her to look at him. "My dearest girl, whatever is wrong? You have not been yourself all evening!"

The gentleness in his voice was too much; the tears rolled faster and she had lost the power to stop them. She was enfolded in his arms and carried across to the sofa where she cried her heart out for all her wasted dreams while he, grim-faced, cradled her as though she were a child and murmured words of comfort. And when all the tears were spent, she was filled with a great echoing void.

"Do you want to talk about it?" Gervase asked softly as she lay quiescent in his arms at last, wracked only by the occasional sob.

But she could not tell him—not out of any sense of shame—for he surely would not need telling that she had not posed for the picture. Her fear was rather of how he would react. In his anger he might even try to kill Sir Hugo and she would not put his life at risk. She said in a muffled voice that it must be reaction after the strain of Cosmo's illness. "And today, you see, he let slip how lonely he is going to be without me!" Her voice, shaking a little, added conviction.

"Well, that is easily settled, dearest goose," he chided. "He can be with us for as long as he wishes—and if he wants to go back to Venice, we will visit him as often as you please, and your engagements permit."

"You are so good!"

"Fustian! I am quite fond of the old man myself." Gervase held her away a little from him. "And that is all it was?"

It was not easy to meet his eyes and tell an untruth, but somehow she managed it. They remained there for a long time, very close, but saying little until at last Gervase declared that they must move.

"Must we?"

Gervase chuckled. "I fear so, dear girl, unless you wish us to be thrown out!"

She sat up, feeling very strange, still holding his hand, not wanting the moment to end. Might not this, after all, be the last time they would be alone together? Her eyes, wide and intense, studied him as though she would store up the memory. His coat was crumpled; she put out a hand to smooth it and a sudden urgency shook her.

"I don't want to leave you!" she blurted out, and saw surprise followed by the faintest of frowns. "Well, is that so shocking?" she added with unwonted truculence. "It seems quite absurd, don't you think, to observe the conventions when we shall soon be together anyway?"

"*I think*, my dearest love," he said with a smile of great tenderness, "that you are very tired and have drunk rather too much champagne. I shall therefore remember that I am a gentleman and take you home before you succeed in seducing me!"

"But I mean it!" she insisted. "I thought you would want it, too!"

"Oh, I do! Never doubt it. But not tonight, I think. Besides"—his eyebrow quirked irrepressably—"however should I face your Tia Giannina if I don't deliver you home safe and sound? I am scared enough of her as it is!"

In spite of herself she uttered a hiccuping little giggle. He dropped a light kiss on her forehead, picked up her wrap, and draped it across her shoulders.

Marissa lay awake with pounding head long after everyone else had gone to their beds. In the end she threw back the covers and padded across to the window, drawing back the curtain to let the moonlight come flooding in. Its brilliance made her eyes narrow with pain, but she stood there for a long time, wide awake, listening to the silence and trying to make coherence out of her jumbled thoughts.

Sir Hugo must be made to destroy those pictures, she decided—if only she could think of a way to make him do so. What she needed was a weapon of some kind. But, of course! Cosmo had a pistol—she knew that he always kept it by him, particularly when they were traveling. If, as they hoped, he was well enough to take his first steps to the drawing room tomorrow, she would be able to look for it, borrow it without his knowing.

With that decision taken her mind should have been easier, but it wasn't. One half of her was relieved that she wouldn't see Gervase until it was over—he was to be out of town for most of the day and she had made excuses for the evening—the other half was terrified that if things went against her, she might never be able to face him again.

If only her head would stop aching, it might be possible for her to sleep. Her reticule lay on the small table by the window. Marissa opened it and took out the vial of laudanum, her fingers hovering over the stopper. Gervase disapproved of it, she knew, but surely, just this once . . . She sighed, and with a tiny shrug, put it away again.

Chapter 15

Elijah Briggs had been behaving oddly all day, following Marissa about like a moon-calf until Signora Tortinallo, falling over him for the upteenth time, lost her patience entirely and banished him belowstairs.

Not that Marissa had noticed anything amiss; she had problems enough to tease her. The scheme worked out with such ease in the dark of night now seemed pathetic. Her knowledge of firearms was negligible and any confidence she might have had in her ability to bring off such a tour de force had shrunk to nothing.

Yet, as the day wore on, nothing of more reasonable nature presented itself. She longed to confide in someone; had Gervase not expressed his intention of riding out to Richmond to visit a friend, she must surely have weakened in her resolve and told him all. As it was, she was so totally immersed in her own thoughts that she scarcely listened to a word that was said to her. Tia Giannina, finding her curled up on the drawing-room window seat alone proceeded to catalogue the whole of Elijah's shortcomings and concluded with the observation that it was not healthy for such a boy to hang onto her skirts the way he did.

"It is as Sir Hugo said yesterday," she concluded forcefully. "If you must harbor such a rude fellow, he is better suited to the stable yard!"

To her astonishment, Marissa rounded on her in a fury to declare that Sir Hugo did not have the say in her house, and never would, so long as she had breath to deny him; after which inexplicable outburst she rushed from the room, leaving the signora to shake her head over such inexplicable passions.

This exchange did much to bolster Marissa's flagging resolve, and it was strengthened still further by an afternoon spent quietly with Cosmo. He had accomplished the walk to the drawing room without any ill effects and for a long time they sat together in total harmony. Every day Signor Pucci was gathering strength, and with returning strength came more animation, a more general interest in events.

"I am sorry," he told her ruefully. "You should now be enjoying yourself with your friends."

"Stupid one!" she chided. "How could I enjoy anything, knowing that you were ill and had need of me!"

His smile was a shade quizzical. "Well, soon you will have no such excuse. Madame St. Austin is in Brighton, is she not? I see no reason at all why you should not go to her once we are settled at Chiswick—after all, you still have your engagement with the Prince to fulfill. When is that for?"

"Not for two whole weeks," said Marissa, reluctant to think beyond the present. But one thing she must broach. "Tell me, how would you feel if . . . if Sir Hugo withdrew his patronage? Would you be dreadfully disappointed?"

She watched his face intently. A slight shadow passed over it, but it was gone in an instant and his face, though grave, was serene.

"At this moment, *cara mia*, I care for nothing except that I am happy simply to be alive. Ambition, I fear, has taken a back seat . . ." He patted her hand. "I hope that does not distress you?"

Marissa shook her head vigorously. "I care about nothing so long as you grow well and strong again!"

"I am naturally gratified. But that does not mean that I wish you to waste your talent. Mr. Maxwell will, I think, be a more than adequate substitute for me, and if Sir Hugo does withdraw, then he will doubtless find a way around the problem." Signor Pucci glanced keenly at her. "Do you anticipate that Sir Hugo will make difficulties, perhaps, when he knows that you are to marry Mr. Maxwell? I know that he had some hopes himself in that direction!"

She made no immediate answer, but he took her silence for assent. "Well, it will be a great pity if he takes the news badly, but it is not the end of the world, after all."

His hand tightened on hers and she looked up to find an unbearable sweetness in his expression. "You are everything to me, *carissima!* You have given me more joy in my later years than I had any right to expect! Whatever you decide, I shall be with you in it."

Moved beyond words, she knelt up and put her arms around him, and in the course of that embrace her resolve hardened. Whatever the cost, he must not be hurt.

Elijah, banished to the kitchens, eventually fell foul of the cook, a voluble Italian of immense girth who resented his presence and made no bones about telling him so. Elijah was unable to appreciate fully the colorful language, but he had no trouble whatever in understanding the message. In his misery he took himself outside and sat on the step to wrestle in peace with his problem.

There was no doubt in his mind that the signorina needed help, but much as he longed to be the one to champion her, common sense told him that he was no match for a flash gentleman like Sir Hugo. As the hours sped by, he grew desperate in his bid to find a solution to his dilemma. It was, after all, a delicate matter of the lady's honor that was at stake—thinking of that picture and all—not something you could rightly confide to someone else, unless that someone thought enough of the lady to discount ignoble thoughts.

Mr. Maxwell—the name flashed into his mind. Now there was a gentleman as seemed mortal fond of the signorina! Yes, of course! There was no nonsense about Mr. Maxwell, though he had a cutting way with him at times. And never a day passed that he didn't come to the house. By a little astute questioning of the other servants he ascertained that Mr. Maxwell hadn't already called that day; and thereafter he haunted those places where he might watch for his arrival.

But Mr. Maxwell didn't come. Afternoon stretched into evening and he didn't come. Elijah began to panic. Suppose he didn't come? Suppose it got to eight o'clock and there was no one to save the signorina but himself? He had caught a glimpse of her a little earlier, and though she was putting on a brave face, he could see exactly how she felt.

A few more questions and he had learned where Mr. Maxwell lived. Without a thought for the trouble he would call upon himself by going off without permission, he slipped out and ran all the way to Grosvenor Square, only to find that his quarry still eluded him. Mr. Maxwell was not at home, said the sniffy footman on the door, nor was he in any position to tell the likes of Elijah what time Mr. Maxwell would be back, though persistence did wring from him that he was expected sometime that evening.

Elijah lost count of the number of times he traversed the Square, kicking at the stones and watching the last remaining brightness of the day dwindle into twilight. He was on the very point of abandoning his vigil when at last he heard a carriage approaching and a moment later a black phaeton swung into the Square drawn by the familiar matched grays. In his relief, Elijah catapulted across the road before the wheels had stopped turning and the alarmed groom, ever mindful of his master's safety, uttered a warning cry and prepared to do battle.

Gervase, however, had recognized the figure racing toward him and assured Wyatt calmly that they were not about to be set upon. He looked down at the panting boy with some curiosity.

"I got to see you, guv, on a very *private* matter!" gasped Elijah with a meaningful glance at the groom.

Gervase lifted a laconic eyebrow and said that Wyatt was the very soul of discretion, but if such reassurance would not suffice, he had better come inside.

"There ain't no time for that, beggin' your pardon—it's what you might well account a matter of life or death, concerning a lady as we both thinks a lot of, if you follow my meaning, sir?"

There was no mistaking the urgency in the boy's manner. "Very well." Gervase held down an imperative hand to him and hoisted him up. "If Wyatt will move over a little we can make room for you," he said. "And you may explain the matter to me as we go. Where *are* we going, by the way? To Arlington Street?"

"That depends, guv—" Elijah saw the gathering frown of impatience descend, and hurried on. "If it's after eight o'clock, then we're too late for Arlington Street and you'll need to make for Merton!"

With quite astonishing forbearance, or so it seemed to Elijah, Mr. Maxwell took a watch from his vest pocket, considered it, and returned it without comment. Then: "Merton, it is," he said in a curiously expressionless voice and whipped up the horses. "And now, my lad, I will have your explanation, if you please, and God help you if you are jesting with me!"

"It's no jest, guv—may I be struck down if every word ain't gospel!" He began to tell Mr. Maxwell what he had overheard and he listened without interruption and without once taking his eyes from the road or wavering in his superb control of the ribbons, which Elijah could not but watch with admiration. Only when he came close to the end of his tale did he falter and at once a quick hard glance flicked him in the gathering gloom.

"You say that Severin constrained your mistress to meet him at Merton, that he issued threats against her and against Signor Pucci, but what kind of threats, lad? You will have to be more specific if I am to know how to act!"

Elijah felt himself going scarlet with embarrassment; it might not have been quite so bad if they'd been alone, but with the groom listening . . . "It's a bit, well, difficult to say, guv—" he began awkwardly, and saw impatience tighten the already rigid jawline. "I didn't understand it all, meself, see, but he had this sketch on him and I guess he meant to have it made into a painting to give to Signor Pucci in place of another one—"

"Did you by any chance see the sketch?"

Elijah was silent, and again the glance flicked him.

"Well?"

He swallowed. "Yes, guv."

"And?"

"I can't say, guv—not wiv him listening!" came the agonized whisper. "Matter of fact, I've got it here, in me pocket—I lifted it from him, see?"

A fleeting glint of amusement lit Mr. Maxwell's eyes. He addressed his groom. "Be so good as to take the ribbons for one moment, Wyatt."

"Yes, sir," said Wyatt, poker-faced.

There was hardly light enough left to see by, but it sufficed. Gervase, after the briefest glance, put the sketch away in his own pocket without a word and once more took control of the reins.

Marissa, traveling some way ahead of them along the same road, felt her stomach churning with awful expectation every time a pair of gateposts showed white in the light of the carriage lamp; each time they passed over a rut in the road her fingers closed on the pistol, hard and cold against her side beneath her domino. She had taken it from Cosmo's room when he was safe in the drawing room and Luigi was belowstairs. Its very solid presence intimidated her when it should have brought comfort. She wasn't even entirely sure whether it was properly primed, and could only pray that she would not be obliged to put it to the test.

She leaned back against the squab and took deep breaths to calm herself. Tonight a superlative performance would be required of her and it would not do to allow fear to get the upper hand. It had not been particularly pleasant to be obliged to practice deception upon her dear ones, but she had shown a capacity for invention that she hadn't known she possessed. Tia Giannina's curiosity concerning the mysterious nature of her journey had led her to create an entirely fictitious friend who was holding an illuminated masked ball in her gardens at Merton.

"I do not know where is this Merton," said the old lady with one of her derisive sniffs, "but it seems a very strange thing to me that this friend, of whom I know nothing, should send a carriage for you when you have your own. Also that you travel without a gentleman for your protection. What is Mr. Maxwell thinking of to allow it?"

"Goodness, how you fuss!" Marissa had managed a

lighthearted laugh. "I told you that Mr. Maxwell was to be away for the day, but I shall be perfectly safe, I assure you!"

All too soon the carriage was turning in through wide gateposts. It followed a short driveway and pulled up before the house, darkly outlined against the sky. The driver climbed down, went to knock at the door, and returned to help her down with a complete absence of curiosity, very much, thought Marissa with sinking heart, as though he had done the same sort of thing many times before.

She was admitted by a similarly incurious housekeeperly woman who bade her a polite "Good evening, 'm," as she ushered her into a compact square hall sparsely but adequately furnished and lit by a pair of lamps.

Almost at once Sir Hugo appeared in the doorway of a room on the right. He wore the black domino draped over his evening coat and made her an exaggerated leg.

"Good evening, Marissa, my dear. Do come in." He nodded briefly to the woman. "Thank you, Mrs. Snape, that will be all."

She bobbed and left them and Marissa walked, straight-backed, past Sir Hugo, glad that she had taken such pains with her appearance. With astonishing composure the hood of the rose domino was let down to reveal the sable hair swept up into glistening curls and her jade eyes glittered with confidence as she looked about her. They were in a small parlor lit by candles and furnished quite pleasantly in chintzes. Her eye was at once taken by an easel draped in cloth which stood in the corner near the window.

Sir Hugo momentarily disconcerted by her ease of manner, observed her sudden pallor. He recalled the sketch which had disappeared sometime between his leaving her yesterday and arriving home. Perhaps she had it and had thought herself in a bargaining position. He smiled at the thought.

"Just so," he said. "Your portrait, my dear. I do have the original, as you will shortly see. But before the unveiling, a drink perhaps?"

"No," she said stiffly.

"Oh, come! What is your pleasure? I daresay I may have some ratafia—or do you feel it should be champagne?" His dry voice mocked her. "This is, after all, something in the nature of a celebration, is it not?"

Marissa swung around, staring, and her hand on the pistol felt clammy. "A celebration?"

"Certainly. I have long dreamed of the moment when you would consent to be my wife!"

"You go too fast for me, sir." She kept her voice steady. "I was not aware that I had consented to anything beyond coming here to view the picture you say you have in your possession."

"Oh, I have it right enough!" He strode swiftly across the room and flung back the cover.

Prepared this time for what she would see, Marissa studied the picture for a moment objectively. It was, without doubt, an exquisite painting, tastefully and cleverly executed, for it was quite obviously taken from life. She said as much in a clear unemotional voice.

Sir Hugo smiled, and shrugged. "One beautiful woman's body is very like another's and in the hands of a skilled artist . . ."

"Oh, he is certainly that," she said. "It is almost a pity to destroy it, but it must be destroyed, of course!"

He looked slightly taken aback by this calm assumption—and then he laughed abruptly. "And so it shall be, my sweeting, the day I make you my wife. We will destroy it together—you have my word on't.

Perhaps I shall commission a study from life in its place!"

The time had come. She took a deep steadying breath and withdrew the pistol from beneath the folds of her domino and raised it slowly, using both hands to hold it steady.

"I fear, Sir Hugo, that I cannot wait for so unlikely an event."

"What . . . !" He stared, uttered a strange, inarticulate noise, and ran a hand across his mouth. "By God! I make you my compliments, Marissa. You have nerve—I'll say that for you!"

"I am not interested in your compliments, Sir Hugo. Nor am I feeling particularly patient. You will please to put the portrait in the fireplace and set light to it."

His laugh had acquired a rasping quality. "And if I decline to do so?" he mocked. "What will you do, my dear signorina? Shoot me?"

Behind Marissa the door opened and a voice cold with rage said, "No, Severin. If you decline, *I* will deal with you—and with more promise of finality, I feel!"

Taken totally off her guard, Marissa swung around to see Gervase at her shoulder, like an avenging angel in his voluminous drab driving coat, and looking more angry than she had ever seen him. She flung herself upon him and felt one arm close around her as she became somewhat incoherent in her relief.

He said with blessed calmness, "I do hope that pistol is not loaded, my love!" and she realized with horror that the barrel was pressed hard against his chest.

She extricated it with a sound somewhere between a laugh and a sob. *"Oh, Dio mio!"* she cried, standing back. "In truth, I am not sure myself!"

His expression was rueful as he took it from her and put it in his pocket. Then, as Sir Hugo moved, he said sharply, "Stay where you are, Severin. I am armed, as you will find to your cost should you try anything foolish." His eyes moved briefly to the easel. "So that is the finished portrait," he said in a considering way. "A pretty fraud, but easy enough to accomplish given a moderate degree of skill with a brush—and a willing model!" His eyes flicked Sir Hugo. "My affianced wife requested you to burn it, I believe? We are waiting."

Sir Hugo was suffused with angry color; to lose Marissa at all was bad enough—to lose her to Maxwell was doubly galling. Fury made him indiscreet. "You harbor reservations concerning the picture, I see," he said harshly. "No doubt you are familiar with the original!"

Almost before the words were out he had gone down, felled by a crashing blow to the jaw. Gervase stood over him with such a look on his face that Marissa rushed forward to take his arm, begging him to desist. "Please—oh, please! You must not, I beg of you ..."

Gervase drew a deep breath and turned to look at her, the expression that had frightened her slowly dying out of his eyes. "Forgive me, my love! I had not meant to scare you." He watched as Sir Hugo struggled up on to one elbow. "Pray, oblige me by going outside where I believe you should find that the coach which brought you is waiting to take you back home." A smile flitted briefly across his face. "You will also find young Elijah, to whom you really owe your safe deliverance."

"But how?"

Gervase saw that Sir Hugo was struggling to his feet to lean heavily against the wall. "Go now, dearest. Elijah will explain it all as he accompanies you home. I will come to you presently."

Marissa glanced anxiously at Sir Hugo. He looked

dazed and was feeling gingerly at his face where a spreading patch of color already disfigured it. She said desperately, "Could you not come now?"

His expression hardened once more. "I fear not. I have business to conclude here!"

He led her to the door where she hesitated, half looking back. "I do not wish you to be hurt..."

"I shan't be," he promised; and as she still resisted said, with more firmness, "Go, Marissa."

And Marissa, seeing that implacable look, obeyed.

The coach was waiting, as Gervase had said. Elijah, perched disconsolately on the step, leaped up at the sight of her, and Wyatt, walking Mr. Maxwell's horses, quietly touched his hat to her and expressed the hope that she had taken no harm.

There was an air of unreality about that journey home. Elijah was vociferous in his relief, chattering on and on as he explained with some pride his own part in the events of the last two days. Marissa was glad that little was expected of her beyond the odd word of praise, for most of her thoughts were still centered upon the house they had left behind, worrying, wondering...

Tia Giannina was astonished to see her back so soon and Marissa, having neither the desire nor the will to deceive her further, said simply that the whole thing had been a misunderstanding. Naturally, so meager a statement did not satisfy the signora. She pursued Marissa to her room, speculating aloud as she whisked her out of the domino and into a loose wrapper, but Marissa would not be drawn.

The signora changed back. "Also, that boy has been missing for all of this evening!" She unpinned Marissa's hair and began to brush it vigorously. "Of course, I have said from the start that he would be unreliable, as well as untrustworthy, but my advice is

214

seldom heeded! It will be marvelous, I tell you, if we do not discover half of the silver to have vanished with him!"

At this point Marissa roused sufficiently to champion her protégé. "Elijah has been with me," she declared, meeting Tia Giannina's inquisitive eyes in the mirror with a look that dared her to comment. "And furthermore, I owe him a big debt of gratitude!"

This brought her mind back to the evening's events and she fell once more into a reverie, only to start violently as the faint peal of a bell came from below. Her whole face came alive with mingled hope and fear as she gathered up her skirts and ran to the landing.

Gervase had not waited to shed his coat before taking the stairs two at a time. Marissa waited at the top, her hands outstretched.

"Oh, you are safe!" she cried, tears of joy springing into her eyes and spilling over unheeded. "I have been through such agonies!"

He kissed her hands and gathered her close, burying his face in her hair. "So little faith!" he chided tenderly. "I am not flattered! Come, my love—all is settled and the picture destroyed, and I have assured myself that the artist will not repeat his error. Sir Hugo will trouble you no more!"

Marissa lifted her head in sudden alarm. "He is not . . ."

"Not dead, no," he said harshly. "Though he deserves to be! But I think London will not see him for some time to come."

He looked up to see Tia Giannina puffing into view. She folded her arms with difficulty across her immense bosom.

"So that is to be the way of it! Not that one is surprised after all those roses!" She fixed them with a baleful eye. "As for tonight—I make no complaint

215

that an urchin brought in from the streets seems to be better informed than I who have nurtured you . . ."

"Dearest Tia Giannina!" Marissa cried. "It is all so very complicated to explain, but you shall know of it very soon, I promise you!"

The signora sniffed.

Gervase gave her his most charming smile. "Five minutes, only, signora!" he begged, leading Marissa toward the drawing room.

She shrugged her shoulder. "And when did lovers ever take so much account of time?" Her black eyes glinted. "Tomorrow will be soon enough!"

About the Author

Sheila Walsh lives with her husband in South-port, Lancashire, England, and is the mother of two daughters. She began to think seriously about writing when a local writers' club was formed. After experimenting with short stories and plays, she completed her first Regency novel, THE GOLDEN SONGBIRD, which subsequently won her an award presented by the Romantic Novelists' Association in 1974. This title, as well as her other Regencies, MADALENA, THE SERGEANT MAJOR'S DAUGHTER, LORD GILMORE'S BRIDE, and THE INCOMPARABLE MISS BRADY, are available in Signet editions.